This story is a work of fiction. Names, characters, places, and incidents are fictitious and any similarities to actual persons, locations, or events is coincidental.

ISBN: 978-1-989206-77-5

UNNERVING

TRANSMUTED

EVE HARMS

PROLOGUE

The thing is attempting to speak, pushing the air from its lungs, which I enlarged to be five times the size of their original human form. My intention was to tune the exhalation tubes that run through its body to play a perfect D Minor, and then a shift to a C Major. It would be an organic pipe organ, a tribute to the quaint church instrument of my youth. But I failed, and instead it sounds like a leaf blower stuck in the mud. I look down at this contemptible, utter failure. "Are you still trying to speak? Perhaps call out for help? It's no use, I've taken away your vocal cords; there's no one to help you, and you're not quite 'you' anymore, are you Greg? Surely you must have some idea of what I did to you?"

The wretched creature gurgles and produces a high-pitched wheeze like the air of a balloon let out while pulled taught. Perhaps it wants to see for itself. I wheel my failure to the mirror, the one with the antique frame I purchased in France on my last research trip. Hand-carved, gilt wood, gorgeous—almost a shame for such a thing of beauty to reflect such a travesty.

The pathetic lump falls silent as it studies its new form. I can't believe I presented this pile of mistakes to the others. I was too ambitious, the human body can only be transmuted so far. And for my hubris I ended up

1

with what looks like a trash bag made of pasty human skin, pocked with red, chapped blowholes, purple patches of discoloration, a bulbous and drooping cartoon nose, a stretched mouth with lips too heavy for the muscles to lift them, and bulging eyes that cannot close. And the rancid cherry on top: a mound of scraggly brown hair that looks as if a child drew it.

The thing is an aesthetic nightmare. It must be filled with horror to see itself, especially with me standing behind it in contrast—perfectly shaped features and flawless skin and all.

But that's not horror in its eyes. Perhaps it's sadness? Resignation to its fate? And indeed, what should be done with this disaster? Surely it's not worth keeping with the others. It would just remind me of my failure.

But I should be reminded. I should look upon this disgrace often, so I will never make such a mistake again. I will display it in my lab next to the others.

I unplug the hose connecting the creature to the air compressor, and its body slowly collapses. Squealing comes out of the air holes, creating an off-key chord as the sack of skin deflates and folds in on itself with the stink of flatulence.

Next time, I will not fail. Next time, I will create an unworldly being of indisputable beauty. Next time, they will know my genius. I will be the one to feed the beast.

CHAPTER ONE

I move my head from side to side, open my mouth and raise my eyebrows. The 3D blue-haired anime head avatar on the screen mirrors my movements. I don't really consider anime girls any sort of *transition goals,* but it's a free model, and it's cute—I'm not really interested in being a T-Rex or a robot.

I don't like showing my face when I stream. My profile picture is a photo, and sure it's liberally FaceTuned and taken at the best possible angle, but it's still technically me so people know what I look like—sort of. But when I'm on camera, I'm too self-conscious, and it's too distracting to see myself in the corner of the screen while I play. And even though this time I'm not playing anything, I'd rather hide and be an anime girl. After a year of voice training I sound great, so showing my clockable face would just ruin all of that hard work, and a lot of my fans wouldn't see me as a woman anymore. But that clockable face…it's today's big topic.

I sort of hate this part of streaming, the 'ask me anything' and 'story time' stuff. I'd much rather be immersed in playing a game, occasionally looking at the chat and talking to my viewers. Isn't that why they watch? Wouldn't they rather watch me make families to torture in *The Sims 3* or waste monsters in *Doom?* But, I promised them an AMA.

I hit the GO LIVE button, sending an alert to my followers. My view count climbs, it's 543 and now up to

3

1,235. I take a deep breath; 2,530 people are watching. Ever since I did the marathon fundraising streams for my FFS, my follower and view numbers have been much higher, but I'm still not used to it.

"Hey, y'all, it's your girl, Isa. First of all, I want to thank everyone again. To all of my subscribers who donated and the other streamers—hgunnerguy, gibbonsThreeTwoSix, pinkEllinator—who shared my fundraising streams: thank you so much. I still can't believe we raised over forty-fucking-thousand dollars! Along with what I scraped together working at my shitty food service job, it's more than enough to cover my FFS—facial feminization surgery. I donated the extra to other trans crowd funds."

I click a button that triggers an animation overlay and the *Final Fantasy VII Victory Fanfare* plays. Three of my Sims characters twerk under disco-lights and the words 'We did it!' in a cheesy 80s font fly in. I make my avatar smile for the camera with crescent anime eyes and shake my head from side to side while giving double peace-signs.

God, so many positive messages coming in, it's hard to believe. And some not so positive ones, too. I click the red button to ban hammer a few assholes and do my best to avoid reading their garbage. I already have a shitty voice in my head constantly telling me I'm not a real woman, I don't need a Greek chorus of internet assholes to agree.

"Uh…I…"

I'm blanking out. The viewer count is up to 6,421

now. Jesus, it's never been so high. I swallow and reach for Squeezy, one of those fleshy bowling-pin alien stress dolls. I squeeze him under the table and brush my fingertips over his round red eyes and nose, it's the next best anxiety fidget to tweaking my nipple—which isn't stream appropriate.

"So, after being on the waitlist for eight months, I'm finally going to have my surgery in a week and a half with Dr. Bayerd. She's one of the best facial feminization surgeons in LA. She's like, an artist. I'm so excited and so grateful—I'm gonna look femme as fuck."

A flurry of painting nails emojis flood the chat. I smile and giggle.

"So, I guess I owe you an AMA. Go ahead, ask me almost anything."

ladygamerbitch69: How long is your recovery?

truestegg: why do you think you deserve this?

Sarai88: You look fine but I donated anyway because you seemed desperate.

KingHairyBallz: ur hot lol wamt sum fuk

g1mp3y: Are you worried the doctor might make a mistake and fuck up your face?

precious-egg: what's your favorite game?

sissyboylovespie: Do you think you'd still have dysphoria and want surgery if society accepted trans people as they are? Isn't "born in the wrong body" a played-out narrative perpetuated by cisgender doctors?

vtrans98: Isn't it transphobic to get surgery to look more like a cis woman? Non-passing trans women r women too. Passing is problematic tbh like what the fuck

truestegg: dysphoria is problematic if you think about it

God, who are all these people, and what are these questions? They aren't my regulars. Maybe they're subscribers of the bigger streamers who promoted me? Randos on Twitter? I tighten my grip around Squeezy— he doesn't mind. "Uh...how long is my recovery? It's two weeks to a month for the major part, depending on the person. It's a pretty big surgery and..."

I jump when I hear the violent buzz of my phone vibrating against my cheap particle board desk. What's the point of putting it on silent when it makes that horrible noise? A familiar feeling of dread worms throughout my body. None of my friends call me without warning unless it's an emergency. The only person who would do that is...Sarah.

The screen lights up, it's my sister, like I thought. She only calls when my dad wants something, who I haven't spoken to directly in—how long has it been? Almost a year? Squeezy flies out of my clumsy fingers, and I fumble with my phone until I find the button to silence it. I sigh with relief when her name blinks off the screen.

"And my favorite game... That's a tough one. I mean... *The Sims Three* is obviously one of the..."

A text comes in and my eyes auto-dart to the little glowing screen. It's Sarah, of course: 'Pick up now! It's an emergency.' It's always an emergency. Jesus, she's calling again. She won't leave me alone until I answer.

"I'm so sorry guys, but I have to cut the stream short. Some sort of family emergency."

Oh god. They want to see my face one last time, dozens of messages begging to see my face. I guess I owe them that, they're paying for the new one after all.

I turn off the 3D anime head for the big reveal of my manly mug. At least I put makeup on and pushed up my pretty big tits that the HRT gods blessed me with. That should offset the mug a bit. I give a double handed heart sign and press the button to cut the stream. My head swims in stress as I answer the phone. "Hey."

"Hey, it's me."

I crouch down to get below the desk, pushing my rolling chair back, it slams into my bed a foot behind me. Squeezy, where are you? I feel around on the scratchy carpet through the dust and chip crumbs. "I know. What's up?"

"So, I realized I never congratulated you for raising all of that money, you're really lucky."

There's the little guy. I crawl out from under the desk—not before bumping my head on it, of course—and open up Twitter. I squeeze the fleshy alien-clown and its red eyes pop out of its sockets as I browse through my feed, wedging my phone between my shoulder and ear, straining my neck. "Thanks, I guess. It was a lot of work, too. The non-stop gaming messed my wrists up for like a month. I had to take a week off work because I could barely make a latte."

"Yeah, that's great. And who would have thought a C-list game streamer or whatever would have given you

7

a shout-out?"

C-list? hgunnerguy is a big deal. He has like millions of subscribers. She doesn't get it at all. "Yeah, who would have thought."

"So..."

I squeezed Squeezy harder and my short, purple, sloppily painted nails dig into my reddening palm. His protruding nose quivers. Sarah wants something. She always wants something. "What is it, Sarah?"

"So, I've been meaning to tell you this, but I didn't want to upset you. Is this a good time? Are you sitting down?"

I stand up, still gripping the stress toy tight. "Yeah, spit it out."

"So, Dad got a second opinion on his cancer. They said it's not stage three, it's stage four. It's spread to his bladder, and he only has a few months to live."

I drop Squeezy on the desk and walk a few feet to what passes for a kitchen in the slumlordy studios of LA. I feel more unsteady than usual, piloting my clumsy body like it's a broken mech. "And when did you find this out?"

"Two weeks ago, maybe three, I can't remember."

"Jesus," I say, digging my hand into a box of Cheez-Its and stuffing a handful of buttery crackers into my mouth. What the fuck is wrong with me, this is why I'm fat. Why can't I cope without stuffing my disgusting face?

"But there's hope. Uncle Tommy told us about an experimental treatment that could save his life. It uses bacteria or something."

"Okay," I say through a mouth full of crackers. Uncle Tommy is notorious for his suspect online research and lame-brained schemes. He got my dad into numerous multi-level marketing scams: supplements, hemp oil, skincare, weight loss products. Last I heard, they were both still hocking essential oils. He's a joke. "That's good news, I guess."

"The only thing is that insurance doesn't cover it, it's really expensive—"

"Like how expensive?"

"Thirty thousand dollars."

Darkness surrounds my vision, like I'm looking through a paper towel tube and a faint ringing grows in my ears. I swallow, my throat dry from the crackers. "Almost exactly how much I need for the last payment of my surgery," I say, my voice hoarse.

"Dad needs that money, Isa. He's going to die without it."

My heart sinks. I pour myself a glass of water in my pink, sparkly goblet and set the ball of entropy I call my body in motion toward the bathroom. My stack of rescued and rehabilitated stuffed animals stare at me from the bed, especially the ones with the prosthetic eyes I bought at an estate sale. I wish I let them keep their normal eyes. "I...I..."

"Your vanity isn't more important than Dad's life, Isa."

No no no I'm so close I need this. Struck by what I see in the bathroom mirror when I open the door, I

9

pause. I've never been able to get used to seeing that thing look back at me. People have been telling me my entire life that it's me, and I'd believed them. After all, if it wasn't me in the mirror...who was it?

But it's not me, it's a fucking flesh prison. Cro-Magnon brow, receding hairline, square jaw, thin lips, beard shadow—I'm a travesty. Sure, I got softer skin and some nice tits from a year on hormones, a decent haircut, and passable makeup skills. And my face did feminize some from HRT. But you can't change bone—not without surgery. And even surgery can't save me from these broad shoulders.

I'm a joke. After all this work, I look like a man, and I'm so fucking ugly and overweight. Look at that double chin. And that goddamned melting clown is looking over my shoulder and laughing. Why would Mitzy give me that painting? And why did I think it was a good idea to hang it in the bathroom? I should take it down.

"Isa? You there? Sor—"

I open the mirrored cabinet door, it's a relief to no longer have to look at my cursed body. "You know this isn't about vanity, I can't live with this face any longer. Every time I look in the mirror...I look like a fucking man!"

"Isa...you don't look like a man. It's all in your head."

She's lying. Always lying. I put my goblet on top of the toilet and take a bottle of Klonopin from the cabinet and unscrew the top. "You don't know what it's like, how hard it is to be in a body you want to crawl out of and leave behind. It feels like my blood is made of acid. And people stare at me, call me a fag and a tranny. It's not just for my comfort, it's for my safety."

"You've survived this long, haven't you? And you're in LA, now. Let's be real, you barely get harassed. You can always save up, Dad doesn't have the luxury of time that you have. He's dying."

I hold the pill in my quivering hand and put it under my tongue. It'll work faster that way. "No. No, this can't be happening."

"I've got to get back to work—the brat's crying about something. Think about Dad. You'll do the right thing, Isa. You always do." She hangs up.

I fumble with the bottle to close it and spill the rest of the pills all over the sink and bathroom floor and down the drain. Of course I will. I always do. He's dying and I just want a new face. There's no other option without me being the selfish bitch. Maybe he'll pretend to treat me like his daughter if I do this for him.

I grip the edge of the sink, my arms trembling. It's not fair. The dark tunnel around my vision turns red and the harsh, high-pitched tone reverberates in my ear drum. Who does Sarah think she is, asking for all that money? And being so rude? And hanging up without even saying goodbye, like she's in a movie or something?

Dad must have put her up to this. He doesn't talk to me in almost a year and can't even be bothered to use my real name and pronouns, and now he wants thirty thousand dollars for some sort of moonshot treatment? He should hurry up and die already.

I scream and slam the cabinet door shut, breaking

the mirror, cutting my palm open. My distorted reflection looks back at me in the remaining shards of the mirror, tears filled with black mascara stream down my red face. I'm such an idiot. So fucking stupid.

CHAPTER TWO

I hug my legs to my chest as I reach out of the fortress of stuffed animals to grab another tissue from my bedside table. Wiping the tears off my face and blowing my nose, I get snot all over my knees and Grins the bear. He doesn't seem to mind, he hasn't stopped smiling since I hot glued my dead grandpa's dentures on to his face. I crumple up the tissue and toss it into a pile with the rest. Hugging Elephink, the giant pink elephant plushie I found sitting on a dumpster in a park, I sob.

This is my third breakdown since I transferred all the money to my scumbag dad. There was so much build up to this surgery, it was everything. And hundreds of people donated, expecting me to get a new face. What am I going to tell them? What am I going to do?

Mitzy wants me to go out with her tonight, to supposedly cheer me up. I can't go out like this.

My phone lights up and vibrates with a call, it's Mitzy. "You almost ready? I'm about to pick you up."

"No..."

"Let me guess, you're in the fetal position crying, surrounded by snotty tissues and squeezing that stress toy you love so much."

"Close." I'd lost Squeezy somehow.

"C'mon, Isa, pick yourself up. What happened fucking sucks, but you need a break from the misery. Come out with me tonight. There'll be weird art and hot art chicks."

"I can't. What if there's someone there who donated? I haven't told anyone about losing the money except for you."

"You won't see anyone, and you don't have to tell them if you do. We're keeping it a secret until you're ready, right?"

"I can't face the world."

"I'll see you in thirty minutes, okay? Love you." She hangs up.

Mitsuko is my best friend. We went to art school together, and after art school we transitioned together. She stayed a painter, I gave it up and now work at a coffee shop and stream video games. She helped me figure out the best sketchy site to get our estrogen and spiro, brings over the junkiest snacks and weirdest movies, and makes me laugh harder than anyone I've ever met. I took her in when her parents kicked her out for being trans, and she was supposed to take care of me when I was recovering from surgery. No one knows me better, and no one gives a shit about me more than her. She's the one I called for support after I had to give up my money.

She also has a way of getting me to go out with her, whether I want to or not. If she shows up at my door, I won't be able to say no, so I better start getting ready. I probably should hang her clown painting back up, too, in case she uses the bathroom.

—

After six discarded potential outfits on my bed, inexplicable 10:30pm traffic, and 20 minutes of looking for parking, we're walking through the streets of downtown Los Angeles. It's like a video game: you dodge fragrant puddles of piss in front of the posh restaurants, avoid homeless schizophrenics raving under the awnings of pawn shops, and brush-off drug dealers who stand under the pretty twinkly lights that adorn the trees. I don't care for downtown. I can't help but see the grime and the years of neglected people and infrastructure under all the set dressing, but if you have a friend who's trying to get ahead in the art world, the occasional excursion is a requirement.

Mitzy and I arrive at Materia gallery, no piss on our shoes this time. She's rocking her finest athleisure: a classic, black Adidas track suit, spotless white sneakers, and her jacket is zipped down to her chest to reveal a gold chain and nothing else underneath. With her goofy yet elegant swagger, she passes her hand across her buzzed black hair and then wiggles her shoulders in a half-dance. Even though she has a fairly masculine voice, and dresses kind of butch, she still passes as a cis woman. She has this ease of walking through this world, a calm confidence—I'm sure being petite and skinny helps. But even when she was getting weird looks early in transition, she rarely seemed bothered by it.

Petite, skinny, and unbothered—I definitely am not. I look frumpy, unable to put together a decent outfit from my closet of questionable thrift store choices, I ended up wearing my usual: a black cami, ill-fitting blue jeans, and a pink dollar-store ball cap to hide my receding hairline that my bangs don't cover when they're greasy. My eyes are red from crying and my makeup is sloppy. Sloppy Isa—like Sloppy Joe, but a person instead of a sandwich.

The gallery is modest and barebones, the walls painted an appropriate white to showcase the art, and the floor is bare concrete. Synthwave music blasts from a speaker mounted on the ceiling, the bombastic 80s synth bass booms with hypnotic oscillation, joined by a crisp square wave solo, giving an imposing vibe of menace, emotional weight, and a feeling like you're about to do something bad-ass. It's hot and there's a faint smell of body odor from the other art goers. We search around the space for the table with free wine, and maybe even some crackers and cheese. There better be one, free wine is a requirement.

Mitzy grabs my hand, and we weave through the socializing art goers to the wine in the back. All of them are fashionably dressed but their clothes don't necessarily look expensive. It's always a game to guess who the secret trust-fund kids are, and who're the hipsters barely scraping by like Mitzy and me. Everyone is nice to each other at these things—maybe because no one can tell who's important or not.

There's no cheese, which is a minor

disappointment, but thankfully there're plastic glasses of red wine laid out on a folding table for us to snatch. We take a gulp of the sour wine before checking out the art. Mitzy makes that cute little "ah" sound after and nods her head to the other side of the room. "That's my good friend, Rayna Kelley. Her work is incredible, we should check it out first."

I've never heard of Rayna Kelley, my best friend's 'good friend.' This isn't a surprise. Mitzy seems to know everyone in LA, and everyone she knows she calls a friend. I turn my head and I'm met with Rayna's piercing yellow eyes. It's all I can see for a moment. They're so entrancing, a solid happy-face yellow, they must be contacts. I blink a few times and shake my head to regain control of myself. She has a severe facial disfigurement—I didn't notice it at first—a deep slash diagonally across her nose, like a sculptor slipped with their clay carving tool and said *Ah, fuck it, I'll leave it in*.

But she's...gorgeous. And so...tall. She must be almost six and a half feet tall. I can't take my eyes away, and she isn't breaking eye contact with me. The heat in my blood rises, and she gives me a big grin before going back to entertaining the small audience she's towering over. Her hair is the color of ink and hangs down past her ribcage, and she's wearing all black: a thin oversized t-shirt with orange bleach splatters and skinny jeans— a sort of artist's uniform. I think she knew what she did to me—what she made me feel, what she left me with after breaking eye contact. I turn to Mitzy, flushed. "She's...she's really hot."

Mitzy laughs and throws her hands up. "I know, right? She's kinda lanky, but don't you just want her to pick you up and throw you in her dungeon?"

"Mitzy..."

"And she knows Kimmi, too," Mitzy says as she orients me in Rayna's direction. "That shirt's from her Fall line. C'mon I'll introduce you, you'll love her." She steps in front of me and makes sorcerous come hither motions as she slinks back.

I shake my head. "No, no way."

She puts both hands on my shoulders. "Don't be such a dork. Let's at least check out her art."

I squeeze the plastic cup, crinkling it but stopping before it cracks and leaks wine on to my hand. "I'm not a dork, I'm like, emotionally devastated, remember? Let's look at the other stuff first."

"All right...all right..." she says, waving me off.

The first piece is bad. Really bad, like a first-year art student bound for a D– from a forgiving teacher bad. Plastic snakes on a grocery store cake with cigarettes sticking out of it on a Roman pedestal that was probably found in the dumpster behind a second-rate studio lot. The icing on the cake says *shitlord*.

Mitzy shakes her head. "Looks like lazy junkie art."

I sigh. "How did this guy even get into this show? Your work should be here. It's so much better."

She slurps her drink, leaving behind a red wine mustache. "I guess the art world isn't ready for a half-Japanese, clown-obsessed, butch trans lesbian Francis Bacon."

17

I laugh and swat her arm.

She dabs away the wine from her lip with a napkin. "Let's see Rayna's work, it's much better than this crap, trust me."

"Okay fine. But don't introduce me."

We head over, Mitzy goes straight to Rayna and I worm my way around her to look at the art. We're almost back-to-back, and I can feel the heat of her body.

The three poster-sized drawings are beautiful, intricate, and strange. They look like they're from old books, but with alien figures and languages instead of people and Latin script. The first has a flask or maybe a test tube. There's a female humanoid figure inside, hairless with faded burgundy skin and a smushed down flattened head that has pointy ears. She has no nose and long, spidery limbs like her creator. Her lack of clothes reveals perfectly round semi-globe breasts. The figure faces forward, one hand pointing to her head, the other toward the ground with the palm out, bleeding a black ichor. A raven sits on her shoulder and a skull is by her feet. Above the glass container she's trapped in is a black sun with red rays.

"...they're inspired by the symbolism in alchemical art..." I overhear the artist say to Mitzy behind me.

The next drawing is similar, the same figure stands inside of a flask. Their arms make a triangle and both palms face forward. Next to them is a goose or a swan, and behind them is the plumage of a peacock. I'm not sure if it's their tail, or if a peacock is behind them. Instead of a black sun, above the flask is a moon.

The last drawing is sort of disturbing. The figure is being eaten by a red bird surrounded by fire, maybe it's a phoenix, and their blood is spilling out, filling the bottom of the container. On top of the neck of the flask is a bearded old man's head, with a sun and a moon on either side of him.

I feel a finger run down my back, making me shiver. I turn around, it's Mitzy. "They're good, aren't they?"

"Yeah, really good." I scan the room.

"She left, you missed your chance."

"I never had one, anyway."

—

The glow of the screen stings my eyes as I scroll through the 300th picture on Rayna's Instagram page from the cocoon of my bed. They have to be contacts, there's no way those are her real eyes. I check the time on my phone. It's way too late, I should be asleep right now.

There's a gorgeous photo of her, and I instinctively double-tap it before swearing under my breath and un-liking it. That photo's like 3 years old! Will she see the notification even though I unliked it? She'll think I'm stalking her. I tap away from her profile to my main feed, but go right back after skimming through a few boring photos. She has over 100k followers, I only have 2k. She follows fewer than 400 people, and there're pictures of her hanging out with celebrities like Kimmi—who's got to be the most famous trans pop star. There's no way she'll follow me back. I tap the follow button anyway and lock my phone, lying down with a huff.

My phone dings and lights up. I grab it and shove it in my face. She followed me back. Shit.

CHAPTER THREE

I'm not surprised. She asked about you after, actually. She saw one of your fundraising streams, Mitzy's text read, responding to the news that Rayna followed me back.

"What? You didn't tell her, right?" I wrote. Oh my god, she knew who I was, and I just walked behind her and pretended she didn't exist.

I'm smacked in the arm, causing me to put my phone down and shift in the orange, plastic scoop chair. My sister Sarah is glaring down at me, the harsh lighting of the hospital room shines above her and stings my eyes. "Are you just going to be on your phone this whole time? Show some respect, Dad's dying."

"I'm not dead yet," my dad says from under a thin white sheet on a hospital bed. He looks more skeletal and bald than usual from the ineffective chemo, and he still hasn't opened his pudding cup on the tray before him... I wonder if it's good pudding. "It's okay, Ian. I'm sure it's not exciting being here."

I cringe but don't bother to correct him, and neither does my sister. He's the worst, he has no respect for me. When did he get like this?

He was actually a pretty good father when I was a

little kid, when he was still fat and mom was still around. He gave the best squishy hugs, would dress up like Santa every year, and he and my mom had an antique store filled with bizarre treasures. We used to do dumb boy shit like toss around a football and go fishing or whatever too. I didn't care for it much, but I was just happy to spend time with him. And those were the sort of things that boys did, weren't they?

After mom left, he got obsessed with dieting and losing weight. He didn't seem interested in me anymore, even as I leaned even harder into the typical guy stuff to bond with him. Once I left, I was the one who always reached out, unless he was trying to sell me supplements or weight loss products—I think the last one was an IMPROVED U combination weight loss and male enhancement pill. And when I came out to him as trans after college, he went from disinterested to intolerable. After all this time, he still thinks I'm confused or going through a phase, and now uses those boy things I did against me like a weapon. To him, it's proof that I'm not really a girl. He managed to convince his entire side of the family, too. He doesn't get that I was doing those things because I thought I was supposed to, and because it brought me closer to him. We couldn't be more far apart now—this hospital visit is the first time I've seen him in months.

"No, it's fine," I say as I adjust my numb ass on the hard plastic, trying to wake it up.

"I never thanked you for the money, Ian," the skinny bastard says—I swear he's emphasizing my dead name.

I look at him, waiting for the thank you. He stares back. "I don't understand why you need surgery and hormones. Your body is fine just the way it is, it's the body your mother and I gave you."

I feel the weight of his disappointment. But this is on him, not me. I transitioned for myself, didn't I? I clench my hands around the side of my thighs and take a deep breathe of the stale hospital air. "If you'd bothered to stick around, you'd have seen how much transitioning has helped me. I've come so far—I'm less stressed and depressed, my chronic pain is gone, I quit smoking, I..."

"It didn't help with your weight, did it?"

Unbelievable. Fucking unbelievable.

"You're my only son, Ian. I'll never understand why you'd throw that away," he says, shaking his head.

Sarah steps toward him. "Dad! What's wrong with you? He—She wants to be called Isa. Even if you can't understand, you should respect it, and you should be grateful. She gave up a lot of money to save your life!"

I almost smile. I guess she's not totally on his side. Dad makes one of those terse, closed-mouth non-smiles and his eyes meet mine. "Thank you."

I swallow. "Yea, sure. No problem."

And I go back into my phone, tuning out whatever conversation my sorry excuse for a family is having while I check my twitter notifications, then my Tumblr messages, then my Instagram feed. Anything to not be here.

A flickering square stops my idle Instagram scrolling. Big, bold letters appear and flash on the screen along with images of beautiful, thin women in bikinis. It reads: *Experimental feminization treatment for trans women. Safe and fast results. Non-invasive. Need test subjects for free treatments. Look how you feel inside. Feminine. Beautiful. Healthy.*

Jesus Christ, Instagram ads are so creepy. It's like it was made just for me. It's so sketchy...but I'll bookmark it anyway.

CHAPTER FOUR

I'm sweating. I'm not this out of shape, am I? What am I doing following through on that sketchy ad? Am I crazy? I'll just check it out, and if it seems weird, I can go home. If he can make me look anything like those before and after photos on his website, then it'll be more than worth it. I check my phone. Argh. I'm late. I'm always late.

Of course the office is in a strip mall. Practically everything in LA is in some sort of mall. The outside is a smog-stained, off-white stucco with faded green trim. A yellowed vinyl banner hangs on the side of the building, it has a blonde woman putting something in her mouth and smiling out at the passing cars of the busy street. Next to her are the words in bold, capital letters: WEIGHT LOSS REVERSE AGING HAPPINESS CLINIC:

A *FREE* VISIT CAN CHANGE YOUR *LIFE*. Above the door in embossed green letters to match the trim is the name of the doctor: Dr. Henry S. Skurm.

I walk in and I'm struck by how clean the place is. The floors, furniture, and interior decorating haven't been updated since the 80s, but they're perfectly preserved and maintained. The lighting is warm and inviting, the office is empty and silent—I can hear my heavy breathing and beating heart. I'm so out of shape. There's a reception desk, it's empty except one of those service bells I hate. Only assholes ring those, but I'm late, so I give it a tap and the harsh tone echoes throughout the room. The tapping of shoes reverberates from the hallway.

It's a white guy in a lab coat, khakis, and a mint green polo shirt. His face is deeply unsettling in its perfection. I can't tell how old he is, it looks like he has zero pores and wrinkles, like his skin is made of matte porcelain. His eyes are a calming blue, his cheeks and lips are plump and a healthy rose color, and his face is so symmetrical, too symmetrical. He's like a 3D model from a video game with graphical capabilities that don't yet exist.

He smiles to reveal perfectly straight, blindingly white teeth. "You must be Isa, welcome."

"Sorry I'm late."

"It's fine, fine. Why don't we get started?"

I follow him down the hall to an exam room. There's a sink with cabinets above it, tongue depressors and cotton balls on the counter, a reclining seat, lights—but then there's a large steel bathtub that looks like a mix between an industrial vat and a hot tub. Pipes coming out of the walls feed into the sides of the tub, and a shining golden orb the size of a beach ball hangs above it. The orb is suspended by cables, and a tangle of thick, multi-colored, electrical wires connected to the top disappear into an open ceiling panel. A computer that looks like it's from the early 90s is embedded in a metal column attached to the side of the tub. What the fuck is that thing?

He puts a smooth, cold hand on my shoulder, failing to offer comfort. "Nothing to be afraid of. It looks unusual, but I've performed this treatment on dozens of ladies like you, with fantastic results. It's perfectly safe."

"But...experimental."

He opens a drawer and pulls out a clipboard. "We're in the final stages of the trial. You're one of the last test subjects before I'll seek approval from the appropriate regulatory bodies. Before we commence, I have some intake questions for you. Please, take a seat."

I sit. "Hit me with it, doc."

He half-smiles. "What is your weight and height?"

I swallow and sigh. "About two hundred and twenty pounds, five feet, six inches."

Doctor Skurm frowns as he writes it down. "A BMI of thirty-five-point-five, I see."

He's a walking BMI calculator. "Is that going to be some sort of problem? I'm trying to lose weight."

"It should be fine. A very nice side effect of this treatment is that you should lose quite a good deal of weight. It can sometimes also have beautifying effects. For example, your nose veers slightly to the left and your eyebrows aren't the same height. It's possible that the treatment will correct that."

I've never noticed that my nose was crooked. I guess you see those things when you're a plastic surgeon. "That sounds great."

"What aspects of your face and body do you find aesthetically inadequate?"

Inadequate? Kind of weird phrasing. "Well, before my FFS surgery fell through, I was going to get a brow reduction, forehead contouring, an eyebrow lift, hairline lowering, and jaw and chin contouring."

He's nodding. "And your nose?"

"I'm okay with my nose."

"It's quite large. That can be perceived as masculine. I can shrink it to be within a typical female range and retain the shape."

I've never had a problem with my nose. But what if it prevents me from passing? This is probably my only chance. "Sure, sounds good."

"What about your body hair and beard shadow? Do you like it?"

"I mean...no? I guess I like having a little armpit hair. Sort of a European vibe, you know? Is hair removal part of the treatment?"

He grins wider than usual. "I can make you as hairless as a Roman statue."

"Okay, sure. I mean, definitely get rid of my facial hair, if you can."

"And your body itself. I noticed you have very broad shoulders and a wide chest. While some women have similar measurements, it's not typical, and less than elegant."

"Yea, but—you can change that? How does this treatment work anyway?"

He stands, puts his clipboard on the counter and washes his hands. "Yes, I can. I can mold you into the woman of your dreams, Isa. Your features will be perfectly shaped. The treatment is non-invasive and non-surgical and is administered in three parts over a three-week period. Your body will change on its own during this time, and the changes will become permanent with the final treatment."

If he can do all of that, can't he throw in a free vagina? I wouldn't mind one. But it doesn't make sense. How could he do all that? "How does it work? Like, what's the technology behind it?"

"While the human body seems solid, it's made of many cells, up to thirty trillion. Within most of these cells is Deoxyribonucleic acid, also known as DNA. DNA is a nucleic acid, a macromolecule that's essential to all life on our planet by providing the instructions on how that life will develop. DNA usually manifests as chromosomes in eukaryotes, and..."

Jesus Christ, it's like he's trying to bore me. I'm doing my best to pay attention and follow what he's saying, but he's basically sending me back to high school biology. High school is the last place I want to revisit, and I flunked biology. That fucking Mr. Geller. I swear he was harder on me than the other students. I re-live a few choice shitty moments from that time before I realize Dr. Skurm is still talking.

"...so while the technology is cutting edge, it's based on tried-and-true techniques."

He looks at me like he's expecting me to say something, but I completely zoned out. "Wow."

"We'll begin, then."

He has me stand up and spread out to take my measurements. My skin crawls as he lays his hands all over my body and says "hm" and "ah." He measures my facial features with one of those tools that went out of style with phrenology and then instructs me to strip naked and get in the vat. "I'll turn away for your privacy. The liquid in the athano—" He pauses and clears his throat. "The liquid in the tub is opaque and I won't be able to see your body."

Usually, I'd rather die than strip in front of a stranger, but I've gotten this far, so I take off my clothes. The coldness of the office presses on my skin, and it feels like the world can see my frumpy, half-manly bod. The liquid in the tub is thick like slime and pitch black. Its goo sucks on my body as I dip in. It's the warmth of piss and smells like spoiled Silly Putty.

"Let me know when you're inside."

My ass hits the smooth bottom of the vat and the bubbling black liquid is up to my collar bone. My hair floats on the surface and tickles my back. I let out a small sigh and stare at the golden orb hanging above my head. "I'm inside."

"Fantastic." The sounds of mechanical whirring and electronic beeping fill the air. "You may experience some unpleasant hallucinations. Let me assure you, you are perfectly safe."

Wait, what? The orb above me vibrates and turns obsidian. A hatch on the surface opens and a mechanical arm with a collar shoots down and snaps around my neck. I cry out and try to pull the collar apart, but it plunges me into the thick goo. I'm holding my breath, squeezing my eyes shut to keep this goo out of my body. What the fuck is happening? Is he going to kill me?

Some sort of liquid rushes out from jets in the side of this perverse jacuzzi, watering down the goo. It's hot—scalding. I'm being cooked alive and want to scream out. It feels like my flesh is melting off my body, but it couldn't be, it couldn't be. The taste of rotting vegetables seeps into my lips, and I open my eyes, the liquid is almost clear now, and I can see my skin melting off—not like candle wax, but like it's decaying. Like one of those nature shows where they leave an animal to rot and speed up the film. I thrash my limbs about, as if that will slow the process. My hand—oh god—all the flesh and muscle is gone. I have a fucking skeleton hand! But I can somehow still move my fingers? This can't be real—he said I'd hallucinate—but he's killing me. I'm sure he's killing me. Does he realize he's killing me?

The liquid in the tub is clear now, and light is pouring in from above. I look up, and dozens of disembodied eyeballs look back at me. They're coming out from holes in the orb, wriggling their worm-like bodies to inspect my rotting flesh. They're descending closer, and their pupils are glowing all different colors. Red, blue, pink, purple, yellow, orange, green, they're glowing hotter, brighter, the glow is turning into beams that shoot into the tub and penetrate my body. The gaps left by rot are being filled with light. My body is turning into glowing, iridescent energy, the colors swirl and mix across my form. The heat dissipates, and the sensation on my skin is...minty.

The brightness above grows, and the orb has become a cool white, like the moon. The colors of my body mix until they turn white to match. It's like I'm made of energy, like I'm a lamp with translucent skin—perfect and smooth with no evidence of rot. Every inch of my skin has an itch that's being scratched. My breasts grow, their shape changing to be more like a cis woman, and my thighs and ass inflate. My dick is inverting. Is it happening? All of these changes at once?

One side of my chest shrinks again, and then the other. My breasts flatten and harden, becoming muscular and manly, like a body builder. The rest of my body follows, and the thing between my legs pops back out and enlarges. No no no no.

The light emanating from me becomes brighter and brighter until all I can see is white. What the fuck is happening? The shackle releases from my neck, and I jump to my feet, bracing myself on the edge of the tub so I don't slip. I pant and shiver and look around the room. Everything is the same as when I walked in. I look down at my body. It's the same as well, with my masculine pot belly and my dainty dangling dick. The doctor is staring at me, and I cover my privates. Is it a look of concern? No. Cold curiosity. "My apologies if the experience was unpleasant. Allow me to fetch you a towel."

I don't say anything. What the fuck was that? What the fuck could I say? Was any of that real? I felt lucid the whole time. And now he can see my naked, disgusting body. I step out and accept his towel and dry off. There's no black gunk, just wetness. He's turned away from me. "You should notice the feminization effects as soon as the end of the week. I've scheduled your second treatment for a week and a half from now, which will be relatively painless in comparison to today, I assure you. Don't hesitate to call if anything comes up until then."

Follow up? I'm never going to set foot in this office again. I finish putting on my clothes and rush out, not replying or waiting for him to turn back around.

CHAPTER FIVE

I'm getting ready for work, and I can't believe what I'm seeing in the mirror. It's subtle, but I swear my brow is not as pronounced, my jaw is slightly tapered, and even my hairline seems maybe an eighth of an inch lower and less of an M shape. Are my lips fuller? I'm not imagining things; I definitely look different. All of this overnight? This...this is fucking incredible!

I wipe the tears forming in my eyes and burst out laughing. Shaking my ass and singing along to Kimmi's latest album, I get ready for work.

I arrive at work and put on my apron, and begin my long shift of barista-ing. The fragrance of the coffee beans is calming, and I catch myself smiling at the customers without forcing it and humming while I make their drinks. I even try to do some latte art and laugh with one of the regulars about my failed attempt. But mid-foaming a drink I feel self-conscious, like someone's watching me, and I look around the coffee shop.

Rayna. She's staring right at me with those yellow eyes, hunched over her sketchbook on the oversized easy-chair that looks normal-sized compared to her height. She's wearing a black t-shirt and jeans, like at the gallery. I give her a smile, and she looks down. Is she looking away because she's nervous? She looks back up at me with a grin. She's not nervous, she's drawing me.

Instead of my usual deep-seated distress at being watched and recorded, there's butterflies. She's so hot, and she's paying attention to me. Should I do it? Should I shoot my shot? There's no one in line, so I grab my rag and start wiping tables down, making my way over until I'm cleaning off the table next to hers. She doesn't take her eyes off of me and her sketchbook. "Hi, Rayna."

"Hi, Isa."

I peak over at her sketchbook, to see how she's rendered me, but I can't get a good look. "It's...it's nice to finally meet you in person."

"Likewise. I hope you don't mind me drawing you."

"It's cool."

She stares and sketches. I swallow. "Maybe you could draw me some other time when I'm not at work? It's a little distracting—and I'm wearing my work uniform. I could put my hair down and wear something nicer for you."

She scribbles her number on the page, rips it off and hands it to me. "I'd like that."

CHAPTER SIX

I get out my makeup bag and pull up a chair to the full-length mirror by the door—I really need to fix the bathroom mirror, the lighting is better in there. I don't need as much foundation as usual, my skin is smoother and dewy, and the hair on my face is so much thinner. The makeup covers it easily after I shave. Put on eyeliner, I swear my eyes look bigger, not in size, but I can just see more of them. Are my eyelashes even longer? I fill in my eyebrows, my brow bone and forehead are still receding, and my eyebrows are a little higher. I line my lips—I think the top lip is more full now—and put on red matte lipstick.

Makeup setting spray mists my face, finishing the job. Looking...pretty good. It's hard to tell if I pass yet, but the changes are such a relief. It's like a weight has been taken off me, I feel so much lighter. I run my fingers through my hair—it looks more healthy and barely needs styling. My hairline is lowering, so I don't have to worry about hiding it with my bangs. I stand up and check out my outfit—a white bootleg Sailor Moon shirt, Chuck Taylor All Stars, and a black jean skirt that I haven't been able to wear in forever. I can't believe I've lost almost fifteen pounds in one week! But I guess that's the most normal change my body's went through since I saw Skurm.

My phone buzzes. It's a Twitter message. I don't recognize the username. Who the hell is *i drink frog cum?* The message seems nice enough, though. "Hi, Isa! Hope it's okay that I'm DMing you, just wanted to make sure your recovery is going okay. I know you said you'd be off social media for awhile while you recover, but it's been over a week since your last post. I can't wait to see the results!"

Crap, they're going to see that I've read the message, and now I have to respond. What am I going to say?

And I have a ton more notifications. On every single app. I shouldn't have stayed off social media so long. All these people, checking up on me and wanting an update. They want to know when they can see my new face.

Rayna sends me a text, she's on her way to pick me up. I post an update telling everyone that I'm fine and I promise to post some pictures in a few weeks when I'm all healed up. By then, the effects of Skurm's treatment should almost be complete. If it keeps going as well as it has been, I'm going to look incredible. I just hope I don't run into anyone I know until then—I'm supposed to be in bed with a swollen, bruised face, and a bandage around my head.

—

Rayna shoves in her last mouthful of pink cotton candy as we walk. Pink crystals of sugar stick to the corners of her neon blue lips. "I thought it was only in eighties movies, taking someone to a fair on a first date."

I can't take my eyes off her lips. "Oh. You don't like the fair?"

"No, it's fine. It's cute. I mean, I've never even been to one before."

Did I fuck this up already? Was the county fair a bad idea? Why didn't Mitzy tell me this was a dumb date idea? I reach into my plastic kettle corn bag and stuff some kernels in my mouth, the sweetness on my tongue gives me a rush and soothes my nerves for a micro-second. *Baby Cakes* by 3 Of A Kind plays in the distance.

"My dad used to take me every year as a kid."

"That must've been nice, having a dad that took you places," she says, tossing the leftover paper cone into the garbage, missing the can.

"Well, we don't talk much anymore."

She grabs my shoulder and points. "Hey! Let's go on that ride."

Carts slowly travel on a track that leads into the sharp-toothed mouth of a giant clown head. Green spirals swirl on its bulging yellow eyes. The sign above it says RIDE ME OR DIE. I don't remember this ride, but I haven't been to the county fair in years. I shudder. "Don't tell Mitzy, but I'm not really crazy about clowns."

Rayna smacks me in the shoulder. "Come on! It's like a demented circus inside of a circus. How meta is that? We have to go."

I don't want to disappoint her, and while psycho-clowns give me the creeps, it's not a serious phobia or anything. "Okay, sure."

I hand a couple of tickets to the carny, and he lets us in with impressive maniacal laughter. I wonder how many years it took him to perfect that? We hop on to the slow-moving, bright red cart made for two and pass under the sharp teeth of the clown head. Rayna puts her arm around me with a mischievous grin as the safety bar lowers down on to our laps, locking us in. Maybe this isn't such a bad idea, after all.

It's dark, hard to see, but I can hear creepy carnival music ahead of us. I offer Rayna some kettle corn. She refuses and rifles into her bag, pulling out a metal flask, and taking a generous swig before turning to me. I can see her snake-yellow eyes gleam from the light growing closer. She puts her arm around me again. "Want some? It's Absinthe. The real stuff, with wormwood."

The real stuff? What does that mean, is this going to make me hallucinate? Is this legal, could someone catch us somehow? "I think I'm good, thanks."

She wiggles the bottle. "C'mon, Isa. The green fairy is calling."

This is probably a bad idea, but it's the kind of thing you do when you're trying to impress an arty-girl, right? I give my most convincing smile. "Okay, sure, I'm game."

I go to take a modest sip, but she tips up the end of

the flask with a finger, encouraging me to drink more. She looks...delighted? Well, when in a demented circus ride, I guess. The burning liquid travels down my throat as the music gets louder, and the first scene of the ride comes into view.

We approach the facade of a yellow and red striped circus tent. An animatronic, mustachioed man in a suit and top hat gestures mechanically into the tent opening again and again. I sigh and stuff a handful of popcorn in my mouth.

"Ladies and gentlemen, boys and girls: Step right up, step right up for the greatest show known to man. Ladies and gentlemen, boys and girls..."

We continue through the tent opening and a wooden figure of an acrobat passes above our head with a cackle, its feet almost hitting us. Rayna laughs, and the chipped and faded figure slides up the cable to its original position. The creepy circus music floats through the dusty air, repeating one maddening bar over and over. Animatronic monkeys with glowing red eyes juggle human eyeballs to the right of us. On the other side, a skeleton wearing a clown suit and a blue afro wig points at us, roaring with high-pitched laughter. We're about to pass through into the next scene, and a taxidermy jaguar bolts out from behind a tent wall with a roar, its bloody jaws coming within inches of Rayna's face. She shrieks with delight and puts her other arm around me, holding me tight, her face coming closer to mine. I stop myself from gasping. With a screech, a rabid, blood-soaked koala jumps out of a trapdoor at me, and I yelp in surprise. That koala was way more terrifying than it should have been—these animatronics are way too realistic. Is it the absinthe?

We pass into the next scene, the music fades and turns into harsh ambient drones. It's a dark tunnel that smells of disinfectant, lit only by stacks of jars that glow green. Deformed fetuses, monkey-mermaids, giant roaches, and other strange creatures are preserved in the jars, along with severed body parts of all species—some mutated and alien. I wouldn't be surprised if whatever sick mind came up with this scene also thought it would be funny to sneak in a real human hand or brain. I wouldn't know the difference. We turn the corner with a little jolt to face a sign made of flashing red bulbs. It reads FREAKSHOW. I take a breath. This probably won't be good.

The circus music is back, but higher pitched and faster paced with feverish break beats behind it— clowncore or something. To our left there's a laboratory set with FRANKENSTEIN, THE UNDEAD LOVER in a speedo lying on a metal table. A mad scientist—she's blonde and voluptuous and not wearing any pants for whatever reason—is pulling a switch over and over, electrocuting him and causing his pelvis to jerk up and down. Next to that is THE PSYCHIC BEARDED LADY, sitting on a stool in an Eastern European embroidered dress. She has a crystal ball with a ghostly face floating in it, and a set of tarot cards laid out.

And to our right is THE FATTEST CANNIBAL ON EARTH wearing a baby blue muumuu. He takes up almost the entire side of the room and is covered in fake blood—or ketchup—and mustard, repeating the motion of taking a cooked human arm from a pile of body parts and putting it up to his chattering, mechanical mouth. Behind him is a wall of ovens with people inside, moaning and banging on the glass to be let out. Jesus-fucking-Christ. To my horror, Rayna apparently thinks this is hilarious and bursts out laughing and pointing. She grabs my kettle corn and starts throwing handfuls of it at the fatphobic caricature. I sink in the seat; she's watched me stuff my face with popcorn all night.

Unbelievable, she's acting so…gross. I thought she was a good person. My shoulders tense, and I cross my arms, but she doesn't seem to notice. We coast into the next scene under an opening with the sign that says THE FREAKIEST FREAK IN ALL OF HUMAN HISTORY! Great.

It's a hall of mirrors. Dozens of Raynas and Isas surround us, their faces and bodies stretched, squashed, inflated in the funhouse reflections. The spectator, the ultimate freak. Is this supposed to be some of joke or artistic statement? It doesn't even make sense.

I sigh and brush the popcorn crumbs off my lap, keeping my head down as Rayna cackles even harder, pointing at her face distorted in the mirror. She turns to me, wiping away tears from laughter. Her outburst fades into a giggle and she notices I'm pissed. Her expression turns to concern and she tries to put her arms around me, but I shrink away.

We're finally through the mirrors, the ride is over. Rayna steps out of the cart and grabs my hand tight, helping me out. She's not letting go. "What's wrong? You're mad."

"You were laughing."

She looks confused. "Babe, I wasn't laughing at you."

I pull my hand away. "No, you were laughing at the giant fat man robot. It's disgusting and fatphobic."

"Oh, come on, he's not even real. No one could be that fat in real life. It's just for fun."

"It's not funny, it's dehumanizing."

She flips a strand of long black hair out of her face. "But I was laughing at myself too, remember? I'm not a bigot."

"That doesn't make it any better." I turn and walk away from her, arms crossed.

This sucks. I really liked her. We could have been something. Maybe she's just ignorant—but that's not an excuse. I caught a glimpse of a part of her I can't ignore. It was cold, psychotic. Ugh. Why does she have to be so hot?

"Wait!"

I sigh and turn around. She jogs to me and holds the sides of my crossed arms with each hand. Her breath is slightly more heavy, and I can feel it, hot and soft on my face, but I don't look up meet her eyes. "You're right. I'm sorry."

I look up at her. She genuinely looks sorry, even though those freaky contacts take away from her sincerity. "You are?"

She slides her fingers down my arms and takes my hands in hers, breaking them free. "I was just thinking like...everyone else. But you're right. I should know better, I got made fun of a lot in high school for my height and face. I love that you challenged my thinking, I don't want to think like everyone else. We're not like them."

I can hear my heartbeat. I swallow my spit. "What...what do you mean?"

"We're artists."

"I...I just play video games."

She brings me closer to her, our bodies almost touching. "Shhhh..."

I look up at her and fall into her gaze. Her neck craned, our faces are so close. Her electric blue lips are so close. She pulls away and grabs my hand and starts running. "Come on!"

I run to keep pace with her until she comes to a halt next to one of the game booths, a ball toss. Her arms wrap around my waist and she pulls me behind it. The chipped wood wall is scratchy through my thin t-shirt as she presses against me and cranes her neck down to kiss me deeply. Her lips are soft and waxy from lipstick. Her tongue wriggles through my lips, into my mouth, and probes at mine until I join in. The divot in her nose brushes against my face as we make out, her breasts resting on top of mine. Her body is so warm. She smells like flowers and freshly baked cookies, it's intoxicating. I lower my face into her soft chest and she giggles as she strokes my hair. Shivers run up my spine and my body flushes with pleasure. It feels so goddamn good. I can't remember the last time I was touched.

She squeezes one of my breasts, caressing over my nipple with her thumb, and my body electrifies with pleasure. God, I love how sensitive my tits are since starting hormones. Breaking out of our kiss, she wraps her arms around me and tightens her grip on my body. She whispers, "Stay away from me. I'll just hurt you."

Her breath is hot on my face. I slowly lean in to kiss her. Our lips almost touching, I whisper back, "Never."

I feel a ball hit the other side of the thin wooden wall, and I let out a shriek. She laughs, blue lipstick smudged across her cheek, and I laugh too. Our eyes and then our lips meet, and we make out until a carny kicks us out.

—

I flop on to my stack of plushie friends and pull out my phone to text Mitzy to tell her the date was awesome. We even went back to her place to drink and make out more. I didn't stay the night, but I think that's for the best. I don't want this to be a one-night stand. She's not perfect, but I really like her.

I compose a quick text to Rayna: *I had a great time tonight, lets go out again soon.* I press the send button. Am I texting too early? The sound of the text being sent quietly whooshes. I let out a breath and a read receipt appears. She read the text already? I roll over to cover myself with plushies and try to steady my breathing. She still hasn't responded. Was it because we had a Sesame

Street moment over her fatphobia, and now she thinks I'm uptight? We made out right after, so that can't be it. I open our text conversation again. She read the message, why isn't she responding? And what kind of psycho turns on their read receipts?

CHAPTER SEVEN

A cool breeze slides across my face, and I put my hand on top of my sun hat in case it picks up. The grass at the park is a bright, oversaturated green and fragrant from a rare night of much-needed rain a couple days ago. The colors look like one of those videos they use to show off the wide-screen TVs at the big box stores. Stepping off the pavement and on to the grass, I catch a glimpse of my smooth leg slipping out of my long floral pool dress. It's such a relief to not have to shave anymore, and I'm loving how my legs are shaping up. I've lost almost thirty pounds now, and my body is firming while I sit on my ass and play video games. Technically, my BMI says I'm still obese, but my curves are smoother and my skin is tighter. I'm feeling so confident I wore a bikini for the first time, to a park that doesn't even have a pool. How basic LA bitch is that?

The air smells sweet. This day is perfect. This park is perfect. Well, except for the murder of crows picking through a trashcan and making a mess. There's Mitzy, at a concrete picnic table, wearing an 80s tank top with a cartoon flamingo in sunglasses surfing, green vintage running shorts, and leather sandals. She's hunched over, painting on watercolor paper, dipping her brush into a cup of paint water. She doesn't notice I'm standing in front of her. "Hey there, stranger."

She looks up and her jaw drops slightly in surprise, still holding her brush. "Isa? I almost didn't recognize you. You look amazing!"

I laugh and I do a little twirl for her. "Thank you!"

She leans back and tilts her head up. "Unbelievable. You look taller—you're not slouching." She leans in. "And you're wearing a bikini? Summer's over!"

I sit down across from her, putting my phone down next to me. The stone bench is cool on my butt cheeks. "I know, but it's also like, eighty degrees."

She puts her brush into her cup of water and leans her elbows on the table, resting her chin in her hands. "You look like you got FFS. I can't believe so many changes happened in such a sort period of time without surgery! Should...should I be worried?"

I blank out for a minute, a trickle of dread seeps into my skull. All I can hear is the musical rattling and cawing of the crows fighting over trash.

She waves both hands in front of her face and shakes her head. "You know what—no. No worrying. I'm just going to be happy for you. You look fucking incredible."

I breathe a sigh of relief and smile. "Thanks."

"So, did it hurt?"

My smile falls a little. "I've never felt so much pain

in my life. And it was weird—super weird. Kind of traumatic."

"Do you have to go back? Or was it like, a one-time treatment?"

"I'm supposed to go back tomorrow and then one more time after that. Honestly, I'm not sure I could do it again. But I'm so close to passing, and the doctor said I could regress if I don't finish the treatment. And he also said it wouldn't be as 'unpleasant' as the first time."

"Girl, you're passing with flying colors. Whatever you had to do, it was worth it."

She's just being nice. I look pretty good, but I'm still definitely clockable. "Thanks. What're you painting? Another melting clown?"

Mitzy looks off to the side and shrugs her shoulders. "I'm obsessed." Her eyes light up and she points in the air. "Oh! I wanted to tell you! I'm going to be in an art show."

"What? That's great news. When is it?"

"In a couple of weeks—the twenty-eighth."

"I'll be there. I'm so happy for you!"

She grins like she just thought of a funny joke. "You should bring Rayna."

I glance at my phone. "She still hasn't texted me back. I don't know what I did wro—"

From nowhere: "Hello, ladies."

We both shriek when we turn to our left, and the crows caw loudly in response. A man is standing next to the bench, it's like he's been there the entire time.

He's a tall, mixed guy with light tan skin, wearing all

black. He looks young, not ugly but a little nerdy, and he's holding a pack of cards. "Sorry to startle you."

Mitzy has her hand on her chest, still trying to catch her breath. "Don't sneak up on people like that! What's wrong with you?"

He smiles meekly and shuffles. "Sorry, I just saw you two lovely ladies from across the park and thought you might like to see a magic trick."

Mitzy throws her hands in the air, her voice raising. "Dude, no! We're gay. Like, super gay."

The sound of the crows is growing louder and more anxious. He looks down at his cards, his shoulders slumped. "Does that mean you don't like magic?"

I give him a smile and peer up at him over my sunglasses. "Look, you seem like a nice guy and all, but we're just not inter—"

His eyes go wide and his cards go flying into the air as he lunges toward me with his hand out. A deafening shriek of a crow is in my ear, I spin toward it and black wings beat across my head, knocking off my hat. The magician tries to slap away the bird as I cover my face with my hands. The bird's talons scratch my arms as it screeches worm breath into my nose. Its beak pecks my glasses, cracking the lens, and they slip down the bridge of my nose. It's going to pluck out my eye!

The magician jumps up on the table, conjuring a deep voice as he kicks the crow with his boot. The bird screams before it flies off, and the rest of its gang follows him into the air. I look up at him, both of us are trying to catch our breath. He looks down at me. "Well, that was weird."

I thank him, and we turn to Mitzy. She's looking down at her painting with her shoulders slumped and fingertips on the edge of the table. The water cup is knocked over and paint water is all over her work. The large boot print of the magician is stamped on the clown's face. She lets out an unsteady breath. "I was going to show this one…"

CHAPTER EIGHT

It can't be as bad as last time. And was last time really that bad? It was just a gnarly trip, right? I wasn't hurt— I've been feeling great. I can't risk losing all my progress. If I do that, this will have been for nothing, and I won't be able to show my face again. No more streaming, the internet will run me off for being a scammer. This is the right thing. I'm doing the right thing.

Dr. Skurm gives me what he probably thinks is a reassuring smile. He lowers the clear yellow plastic dome over my head and his smile twists and ripples, distorted by its surface. Is his grin growing wider? Or is it just an optical illusion? "You may feel some pressure."

I grip the sides of the chair as the yellow plastic rotates and softens and lengthens, like molten glass. I scream, it covers my head and neck and forms around it, taking the shape of my face and cutting off my oxygen supply. I can't close my mouth and I can't make a sound;

my head is being vacuum packed like frozen fish. Is it filling with water? The taste of salt stings as a thin film of liquid dribbles into my silent screaming mouth. My eyes burn.

I feel a needle pierce my crown, and all the flesh on my head expands against the plastic cage, pushing up against the now hard surface. My eyelids inflate like balloons until they swell shut, leaving me blind. They're pressing into the plastic, my head is going to burst! I'm still swelling, my head presses against the tightening yellow shell and my enlarging brain presses up against my shrinking skull. This can't continue, something has to give, I'm going to explode and implode at the same time—I can't breathe, I can't breathe I can't take this anymore. I'm falling, falling, I'm squeezing out into the dark abyss, falling into my blindness. How long has it been? Seconds? Minutes? Hours? Days?

Light peeks out from the darkness as my eyes deflate. The yellow plastic shell surrounding my head is softening and loosens its grip. I can breathe again. I can see the room, blurry behind my crusted eyes and warped and sepia behind the yellow plastic.

Dr. Skurm is still standing in front of me, smiling with his powdered, porcelain doll smile. That sick fuck, was he watching me suffer the entire time?

He lifts up the dome, and I gasp for breath. He picks up a hand mirror from the counter and shows me what I look like. I'm a little pink, but my features are even more feminine than when I came in. My jaw is more tapered, my brow bone has receded, and even my eyebrows seem to be higher. My lips are fuller and my nose is more dainty. The double-chin is completely gone!

"The pinkness is temporary," Skurm says, "it'll even out in the next few days."

My head throbs and tears well in my eyes.

"And your features will further feminize and beautify in the coming days. You should also continue to lose weight until you're pleasantly trim. There's only one more procedure—a simple injection—and the changes will become permanent."

I'm so close. I definitely pass now. Once the pinkness is gone, maybe I can show my face to my followers and tell them I got the surgery. The results are undeniable at this point, and they're waiting. They want to see me. I'm getting dizzy, lightheaded. I try not to faint.

CHAPTER NINE

I pull up my black work jeans, and they're baggy on me— the legs are too short. This is ridiculous, it's like they're capris. I want to tell myself that they shrunk in the wash, but that would just be a way to deflect from the fact that I seem to be going through my third puberty. First boy puberty, then girl puberty, and now...mutant puberty?

Maybe that's a little dramatic, but looking in the

mirror, things are getting weird. I'm still losing weight, but my arms and legs are longer. I'm not imagining it! I grew two inches taller, almost overnight. My skin looks...healthier. It's a bit more tan with a rosy glow, like I've been exercising regularly.

I trace my finger along my facial features to see if I can detect any further changes. Are my ears longer? My lips fuller? My fingers. They've absolutely extended! This is so freaky, but I sort of like it. So femme, so thin. I'm starting to look like a model, and totally cis. I go back to the bathroom to brush my hair, and my phone buzzes on the bathroom sink. The screen lights up with my sister's name. I accept the call and hit the speakerphone button.

"Hello?"

"Isa, it's me."

I run my brush through my messy hair. "What's up? I'm getting ready for work."

"Bad news about Dad. It doesn't seem like the treatment is working."

The brush gets stuck on a tangled clump. "Great. Well, we knew it was a long shot."

"Yeah. And he's not doing so well."

I tug on the brush, it's still stuck. What does she want me to do about it? Didn't we all know this was going to happen? "I'm sorry, Sarah. I wish I could do something."

"I need you to visit him. As soon as you can. I'm not sure how much time he has left."

I tug the brush harder. "Jesus. Does he even want to

see me?"

"Of course he does. Go see him, I know you'll regret it if you don't."

"Fine." I pull the brush down with all my force and hear a tearing sound. A massive tangle of my hair is stuck in the bristles. "Fuck!"

"What is it?"

So much hair! Did it leave a bald-spot behind? "It's...agh. Nothing."

"Go visit Dad."

"Yea, got it. I gotta go."

I hang up and inspect my head in the mirror. Fuck, that spot on my head is thinner now. How did come out so easily?

My phone screen lights up again. It's Rayna! Finally. She responded: *Let's go out again.*

CHAPTER TEN

I check myself in my phone screen, hoping the Uber driver in the front seat isn't judging me. There's something weird going on with the changes. My eyes look bigger, and my ears are more pointy at the ends like I'm cosplaying a fantasy elf. It's cute, but I don't remember 'elf ears' being on the menu. I just hope they don't get anymore elf-y. My nose is looking thinner and smaller. It sort of tingles. I give it a gentle wiggle and run my hand through my hair. More than a few strands are left behind between my fingers, and I panic and stuff them into the pocket behind the driver's seat. This hair loss is the most concerning, my hair must be thinning. If I lose my hair, I don't know what I'd do.

The car stops and the driver looks back at me. "We're here, miss."

I step out of the Uber, for once remembering to hunch down so I don't bump my head. I'm probably almost 5'11" by now, and I have no reason to believe I won't keep changing. I wonder if I stayed still and stared if I could see myself growing taller. And I've lost so much weight. I eat and eat and can't stop losing.

I'm getting a lot of looks. What do they see? Do they think I'm hot? Strange? Strangely hot? Hot-ishly strange?

I'm on time to the restaurant to meet Rayna for our second date. She wanted to pick the place this time. You can tell this place is fancy because it doesn't have a sign—its name is the address. You wouldn't know it's a restaurant unless you looked through the window at the patrons, sitting around white tablecloths and picking at their food. Was I stupid to take her to the fair when this place is her idea of a date spot? She must have thought I'm low-class or something. How am I going to afford it if she wants to split the bill? Or...does she expect me to pay? I take a breath and push open the large brass double-doors.

The host looks up from his iPad and smiles at me. "Miss?"

"I'm meeting someone here. Um...Rayna Kelley."

"Yes, of course, Miss. Right this way."

Ah, 'Miss,' I'll never get tired of hearing that. The place is crowded, one large room with no nooks to hide in, and the lighting is terrible. It's far too bright, everything is exposed, making it feel less like a fancy restaurant and more like a cafeteria. There's no music, and it's pretty quiet for how many people are here, especially for Los Angeles. Most are focusing on their food and talking in hushed tones. The host leads me to a table in the center of the restaurant where Rayna is waiting for me, looking at her phone with her legs crossed. She's wearing her usual: worn designer black t-shirt and jeans, but has on hoop earrings, red pumps, and bright red lipstick. Am I overdressed? How is she going to react to the changes? Is she going to laugh or be disgusted? Or maybe she'll be concerned? Will she still want to date me? At least I gave her a vague heads up over text, so it wouldn't be a total surprise. "Uh...hey."

Rayna looks up at me without recognition. She sets her head back and her mouth opens slightly. Her voice is low to match the noise level of the other patrons. "Isa? Oh my god, I almost didn't recognize you."

"Yea, I told you it was a lot."

"I assumed you were kidding or exaggerating—but you look great."

Should I sit down? "Thanks."

"So, this is from your surgery? I thought that was only on your face."

I sit down. She's ordered me a glass of wine, so I take a sip. "The surgery fell through, but I found an alternative. It's some sort of feminizing gene-therapy, I guess. The height gain was a surprise."

"It's hot. And your face looks incredible. Maybe it's a blessing in disguise, losing all of that money."

I didn't tell her about losing the money. Did Mitzy tell her? Goddammit Mitzy. The waiter appears and takes our orders, I go with the steak—might as well, this meal is going on my credit card anyway. She orders a fancy seafood soup; I wouldn't know how to pronounce it.

Our conversation is strained and awkward, and I'm relieved when the food comes. The steak tastes as expensive as it is, perfectly cooked and juicy. I must be hungry because I'm eating fast. Too fast. A chunk of meat gets lodged in my throat. Fuck! I put my hand to my throat and grab my water with the other hand. Rayna puts her spoon down and stops whatever she was going to say. "Are you okay?"

Water dribbles out of my open mouth as I try to wash the piece of steak down and tell her I'm choking. It's not working, I can't breathe. She's calling for a waiter to help. My whole face hurts. A waiter is behind me, his arms around me, squeezing violently. The pressure of his thrusts ripples throughout my entire body, pushing into my neck and head. He squeezes again, the air in my lungs pushes up against the stuck food, but it doesn't budge. My head is pounding, and I can see through my blurry vision every diner staring at me. They're all watching me die. I close my eyes. He squeezes once again, harder, and it dislodges the piece of meat. It flies out of my throat.

I collapse into my chair, surrounded by horrified onlookers. God, how embarrassing. I raise my hand and glance around. "I'm okay, everyone."

The man at table the across from us grabs his napkin and lifts it to his face, just a little too slow to catch all of his vomit. The woman at the table next to him points at me and laughs like a chipmunk. Rayna's jaw is tight and her brow furrowed. "Isa..."

She tilts her head down, entranced by her soup. There's a detached nose floating in the white liquid among the prawns and clam meat. I touch my face, and there's a small divot where my nose used to be. That's my nose in her soup!

I scream and the woman stops laughing. Everybody's watching, everybody can see. I don't have a nose! I have to get out of here!

Grabbing my purse and pushing away the waiter, I run out the door, ignoring Rayna's calls for me to stay. I have to go home, I have to be alone. No one can see me like this. No one can see me like this.

CHAPTER ELEVEN

I'm lying on the floor of my apartment in a pile of my hair. I've been here for hours, watching my feet inch further and further away, watching my arms lengthen. It's slow. But I can see it. I can feel it. My skin feels taut with the unending sensation of a downward tug. Can I hear it? The creaking, stretching sound just before an elastic band snaps? Last time I measured myself, I was six and a half feet tall. And I keep growing.

My phone has been dinging and ringing all day. Don't they know I'm busy growing? Mitzy's asking why I missed her big show. The fans want me to do a face-reveal stream, some of them sending death threats, and calling me a grifter, and telling me I'm ruining their life because I haven't done one yet. Rayna is checking in on me. Sarah wants to talk on the phone, whatever she wants to tell me is too important for text. Maybe they need more money.

And fucking Dr. Skurm's office keeps sending me reminder messages. One of them even said, "Part of the final visit is to address and remedy any side effects that may have occurred." He fucking knew what he did to me. He probably lied about testing this treatment on other girls. I must be the first—the only one stupid and desperate enough to answer his sketchy ad. And he used me as a sacrifice for him to figure out his technique. He knew I was going to be a failed experiment. Or this is how he wants me to look, and he gets off by turning trans women into monsters. It doesn't make sense, it can't be real. This can't be happening. None of this makes any sense.

Someone's banging on the door.

Maybe if I just ignore them, they'll go away.

They're knocking harder.

Can't they see I'm growing? Don't they know? I raise

my hand in front of my face, turning it back and forth over the backdrop of my popcorn ceiling. My fingers are so long now. They must be longer by half. I roll them, making a wave.

They're banging on the door, harder.

I run my hand over my head, it's flattened and smooth. The last of my hair fell out. I'm fucking bald. Tears well in my eyes, and an alien, raspy moan slides out of my throat.

"Isa, it's Sarah, open the door! I can hear you growing in there!"

She can hear me growing? How does she know I'm growing?

Sarah is knocking again. "Stop moaning and open the door, I need to talk to you."

Moaning. She said moaning. She can hear me moaning. But she can't come in. "I can't, you can't come in!"

What's happened to my voice? It's strained and lower and darker and more resonant—like a fucking man, like my old voice. Did the changes make me lose all my muscle memory from voice training? My neck looks longer, but have my vocal folds themselves changed? And why wouldn't they have? The entire quality of my skin has changed, it's smooth like a dolphin, my ears and chin are stretched and tapered at the tip, my eyes are huge, and my boobs are looking unnatural, like implants.

"I'm coming in, I brought the emergency key."

Shit, the emergency key! Why did I ever think that

was a good idea? I hear the jingle of my sister fumbling with her key ring. I can't let her come in. I try to jump to my feet, but my knees buckle. They swivel on the joint sharply to the left, like an action figure's leg being yanked, and I fall back on to my boney ass. My stick-thin legs dangle above me, they aren't pointing in the correct directions. The right one is facing backward, and the left one is twisted all the way to the side. I grab my left ankle with my left hand, but it slips out as my elbow collapses with the impact. The bottom of the leg is pushed into a position halfway to normal, but now my forearm is facing the wrong way.

I hear a key entering the deadbolt. I steady my breathing and correct my left arm with my right. Then I use both hands to correct my legs one at a time. The deadbolt unlocks. She can't come in. I can't let her come in.

I rock forward and plant my feet, rising on to my wobbly legs—it's like the reoccurring dream where I've forgotten how to ride a bike. I take a step forward, catching and steadying myself before my knee buckles again. The step was too wide, I'm not sure if I can take another one without falling. The key turns in the lock, she's going to open the door. I'm only a few feet away, if only I can put on the door chain. I can do this.

I launch myself forward, taking my second step. It's a beautiful landing, and I launch off again. But I stumble forward, my pelvis slams into the base of the door, closing it just as it's opening. My testicles ache from my crotch smashed up against the hardwood door, and my spine must have folded backwards because my back is straight, and I see the ceiling and the balls of my feet dig into the back of my head. I swing my upper body with a straight back, pivoting like a crank, and slam into the door as it opens and shuts and opens and shuts, again and again. Sarah does not give up easily. "Let me in, Isa! Let me in!"

I'm able to put the top of my body upright. I can reach the chain without standing, but I'm having trouble holding the end of it, Sarah gets the door open a few times, and it keeps slipping out of my fingers like the tiny clasp of a necklace. She's pushing harder, making exasperating cries. The end of the chain is finally between my thumb and index finger. I shift the entire weight of my body to keep the door closed as I prod to find the hole to stick it in. It clicks into place and I slide it across. I collapse in exhaustion and roll away from the opening of the door. Sarah shoves the door open, but it catches on the chain, only opening a few inches, and she screams in frustration, "Goddammit, Isa!"

She can't see me. She can't see me, and she can't get in. Thank god. The taste of metal fills my mouth, and I wipe it, smearing some sort of brown fluid on my arm and cheek. I make the inside of my mouth and throat as small as possible to attempt to approximate my voice. "I'm sorry, but I just can't let you come in. It's hard to explain." She rakes her nails down the door in defeat, and a sob escapes her throat. Why is she even here? Why won't she leave me alone? "Why're you here? What do you want?"

Sarah makes a choking sound before she takes a deep breath and says, "Dad died, Isa. He's dead!"

The word 'dead' morphs into a yell and heavy sobbing. The kind of loud crying that sounds like a perversion of laughter. I instinctively hurl my body toward the opening, wanting to give her a hug, forgetting my appearance. When she sees a glimpse of my face, she screams, shredding the oxygen in the building to pieces.

Her hand covers her open mouth, and she slowly retreats before turning around to run down the hallway and stairs.

CHAPTER TWELVE

I wake up and he's standing over my bed, his latex gloved hand holding a syringe of green liquid that glints in the moonlight. He presses the stopper, and the florescent fluid squirts out, splattering on his mint-colored surgical mask and cap. His large, mirrored goggles reflect my terrified expression. "You're awake. You never came to your final appointment, so I decided to pay a house call."

Doctor Skurm grabs my arm—how did he get up here, it's the second floor? I try to squirm out of his grip, but he tightens it and steadies the syringe toward my shoulder. "Hold still. This will put you to sleep so I can take you in for your final treatment."

I swing my right arm and sock him in the head. He shrinks back, and I jump off the bed, but my limbs don't bend in the directions I expect, and I collapse on to the floor like a plastic skeleton. Shit. I should have practiced walking more, but I was just so, so tired.

I'm back up on my feet, but he is too, and he's blocking the exit, and I don't think I can get past him. The only other exit is the window. I turn around and throw it open and try to climb out, but he pulls me back by the waistband of my PJ shorts and pins me to the wall. My body is horizontal to the open window as he pushes himself against me, trying to get me still enough to inject me with whatever the fuck is in that syringe. In an attempt to get him off me, I flail my lanky limbs wildly, swiveling and bending them in every direction. Maybe more of my joints have the same freedom of movement, like my hips—or I'm flexible in other ways. I let my body go limp, and fold and slip out of the window from the force of his push.

I'm falling. Sticks scratch my back and pierce my thin pajama shorts and t-shirt as I land into the bushes outside. His masked, goggled face looks down at me from my apartment window, his empty hand reaching toward me. He must have dropped the syringe. He disappears—I need to get up before he reaches me. How will I position my arms and legs so I can run away? God, I wish I had a car. The front door to my apartment building opens. It's him.

I bolt to my feet, but he's already behind me,

wrapping his arms around me in a bear hug. "Fine. We'll do this the hard way."

I twist my arms behind me and try to strangle him from back of his neck, I kick my bare feet in the air, but I can't seem to get a grip or wrestle out of his. He drags me to a white van parked close by; the back doors are already open. It's empty with no seats and separated from the driver with a metal mesh cage. He pushes me in and locks the door behind me. Where is he taking me?

We're moving now, my street fades into the distance in the tinted windows of the backdoor. I bump my head as I stand into a squat—my new height doesn't give me much room—and go for the handles. I pound my fists on the door and rattle the handle. He accelerates and takes a sharp left turn with a screech, slamming my body into the side of the van and knocking me down into a tangled mess. He's driving faster now.

I hear the chiming of a railroad crossing arm descending, and the harsh beep of a metro car. He's speeding up, is he trying to beat the train? I tumble backwards when he slams on the breaks. With almost no fat to cushion myself, my body bruises to the bone. He wasn't able to cut the train off, this is my chance. I scramble to the back window and slam my hands on it and scream as loud as I can, trying to get the attention of the few pedestrians milling about.

They're ignoring me or they can't hear over the train crossing noise, but the middle-aged Latino man tending one of those bacon-wrapped hotdog carts seems to notice something is wrong. I scream louder and pound harder, and I think he realizes what's happening. He bends down behind his cart and comes back up with a propane tank the size of a watermelon. He runs toward the van and slams the tank into the window—is the force going to cause it to explode? The window cracks into a spider web formation, and I step back. The man strikes it a second time—the window's still not broken. The van's engine revs and the train is almost past the intersection. He strikes it a third time and the glass shatters, I reach my arms out and his hands wrap around them with a powerful grip, I'm being pulled away, the van is moving again. His grip is steady, but the window is so small and my head is out but my shoulders are stuck. I take a breath, loosen my joints, and they fold backward like a tripod closing. Squirting out of the window, the glass shards scraping across my body and snagging on my clothes, I fall into the arms of the hotdog man as Skurm's van drives away.

I'm crying and I look up to my savior. His jaw is dropped and his eyes are wide. Imagine what he sees: a bald freak with no nose, pointed ears, Furby-sized eyes, a flat head, and spidery arms and legs. And I'm practically naked, wearing only a thin t-shirt that my nipples show through and PJ shorts with no tucking panties, both ripped and stained with blood from the shattered window and fall. My bulge is obvious in these shorts, but considering the rest of me, they probably won't notice it.

I regain my footing as he pushes me away. Bystanders have stopped to witness the drama unfold.

They're wearing looks of pity, confusion, and terror. I run. The man calls after me in Spanish. Maybe he wants to help, but I just need to get away from here.

Where can I go? I can't go home. Rayna. Her house isn't far. I can get over my embarrassment from the other night, I don't have any other options. Mitzy is mad at me and might not answer my call, I need to get to a safe place before Skurm tracks me down.

I run, the uneven LA sidewalk cuts up my bare feet, and causes me to trip and tumble to the pavement. But I get up, again and again, and keep running. After each tumble, I understand my body a little better. The warm, dry night air flows through the holes in my clothes. Her place is behind one of these three houses. I think it's the middle one. There's light coming from behind the gate, and I open it as quietly as I can, unlatching it easily by sticking my arm through the bars. I steady my breath. What if this is the wrong house?

Rayna sits on the metal lawn furniture under her bungalow's porch light, entranced by her sketchbook, creating worlds on the page. I clear my throat and say her name with my transformed voice.

She looks up and gasps, dropping her sketchbook to embrace me. It hurts, I'm more bruised and banged up than I thought. "Please, not so tight."

"Isa, what happened to you? Are you okay?"

She brings me inside her little one-bedroom cottage, it's small but tidy and comfortable: earthy colors with folk art on the walls, lots of plants, and carefully chosen and placed furniture. It smells like cookies. Are there cookies? I could really use a fucking cookie right now.

She sits with me on the bed and I can see her true eye color under the soft light, a warm brown. Her compassion and concern is exposed without her contacts. "What happened?"

I tell her. She cleans my wounds, changes my clothes, and holds me all night until I almost forget what I've become.

CHAPTER THIRTEEN

I wake up to yellow eyes fixated on me. My body aches, but the clothes Rayna gave me last night are soft and clean. She's drawing me. I touch where my nose was, causing a phantom itch and tears fill my eyes, blurry from sleep. My voice is low, unrecognizable: "Please, don't draw me. I'm a freak, I'm a fucking freak."

Tears stream down my cheeks and my chest aches. I cover my face with my hands, my fingers have grown so long they can almost hide me completely. Rayna's fingertips touch my wrists and she lowers my hands, her beautiful face close to mine, her hot steady breath on my lips. She's wearing only a thin white baseball tee with no bra or pants. Her panties are bright red, her thighs soft and pale like cream. I can see the warmth and compassion of her gaze, even through those yellow contacts. She smiles slightly. "You're gorgeous. I mean it. Let me draw you."

God, she's so nice to me. And hot. Maybe I'm hideous, but maybe she really believes what she says. She's a weird artist chick with a facial disfigurement, so why not? We could be disfigured together, a malformed Beauty and me, the Beast. We could stay in this bungalow and never leave and forget about the outside world. She strips me of my shirt and kisses me. Her fingers run along my back and up to my breasts, she squeezes them gently. Her hand runs down my body to my shorts, and she tucks her fingers in the elastic waistband. Blood rushes to my pelvis. I don't want her to see it, but it's not like she doesn't know I have one. I let her take off my shorts, and she kisses me with her soft, plump lips as she strokes up and down my long legs. She takes her kiss away and stands up. "Let me draw you."

I sigh and nod and let her put me into a pose, reclining on the bed. I insist on covering up my dick with the blanket. She sits back down in the easy chair and sketches my freakish form. Why am I letting her do this? I could be blinded by my attraction to her—but for now, I don't care. "Just...just don't show anyone the drawing, okay? It's just for us."

She smiles. "Just for us."

The way she's looking at me as she draws, it's like she wants to tie me up and have her way with me. She's a welcome predator and I yearn to submit, to be devoured. The red-hot tension grows and fills the space between us. She stops and examines her work before looking back at me—like I'm a person again, not prey or a subject for her art. "Hold tight, I have something for you."

She goes into the next room. I'm still posed, and it's kind of chilly. Where should I look? What am I supposed to be doing? Is she done drawing me? I thought we were about have sex, but it seems like the moment's over, so I put my borrowed clothes back on. It feels weird to hang out naked without the glow of an orgasm for company. I wonder what her drawing of me looks like?

Before I can get up to take a peek, she returns holding a jar filled with formaldehyde. My nose is floating and bobbing inside. "I rescued her for you."

"You kept it?"

She bends down and hands me the jar. "It's a cute nose—you look better without it—but I thought you might want to have it back."

It floats there in the green liquid, slowly spinning. My stomach turns in knots. There's no way to reattach it, it's too late, I'll never look normal again. "Thanks."

What am I going to do with this? Where would I even keep it? I put the jar down by the bed and when I sit up, her face is right next to mine again. She kisses me, and I return the kiss, but I can't match her passion. Taking my hand, she traces my long fingers. She brings them up to her face and rubs her cheek against my hand. Her tongue slides out of her mouth and swirls over my palm, traveling up to my fingers, licking in-between them and up and down them. She's sucking on my index finger, taking it deep into her mouth as she locks eyes with me, and her tongue's tip follow my fingerprint. Heat grows in me, my brain crackles with electricity, and an aching pressure builds in my loins.

Taking off her shirt, she exposes her beautiful bare chest, and puts my hands on her breasts, squeezing them and encouraging me to play. They're soft, so soft. She leans in and her nipples graze mine as she kisses up my long neck, taking off a bandaid and softly licking one of my wounds. Her wet tongue traces my ear and she sucks on the pointed ends, sending bolts of pleasure from the top of my head down my spine and out my toes. She takes my head in her hands and smiles at me. "You're the most beautiful creature I've ever seen."

I try to turn away, but she keeps her hands on the sides of my face. She pulls me in for a kiss, sliding her tongue through my lips, prodding mine, inviting it in. I extend my tongue into her mouth, and she wraps her lips around it and sucks. I relax and let her take it in further, finding I can keep extending it. She pulls her head back, drawing my tongue out as she sucks, her eyes filled with delight that it's much longer than we thought. It drops out of her mouth, and we can see it in it's full length. It must be six inches out of my head. She's smiling bigger than I've ever seen. I retract my freakish tongue, but she grabs it with both hands before I can get it in my mouth and shakes her head no. "Let me love you. Let me love every part of you."

I relax, and she releases her grip, letting my massive tongue lay in her hand like a slug. Rayna gazes at it, pivoting her head to take it all in and then closes her eyes and licks it up and down. She takes it into her mouth again, it slides down her throat before she pulls it out and giggles.

She takes off my shirt and kisses my face as she strokes my dolphin smooth, flat head. Her tongue circles around where my nose once was until she presses her plump lips against the spot. The tip of her tongue touches my nose hole and I turn away. It's disgusting, my face is disgusting.

She takes my hand as I'm turned away and lifts it to her face, putting my fingers on the deep groove that bisects her nose. I turn back to her, her eyes soft and her smile sweet, and I stroke her deformity. "How...how did it happen?"

"My dad did it to me."

I pull my hand away like I touched a hot stove. "Oh, god. I'm so sorry."

Rayna smiles. "It's okay, he apologized. And it makes me who I am. And I'm fucking hot, don't you think?"

"Yes. Really...really...hot."

"Suck my tits, Isa. Lick them with your freaky tongue."

We laugh at the outrageous statement as she flops on her back. She pulls me to her and I lick her breasts, my tongue wraps around each one and flicks her nipples. She moans as she takes off her panties and pulls my head down to her crotch. My tongue surrounds her button, moving in circles, and she pushes my head closer. Rayna pants and screams in pleasure, almost sounding like she's going to break out into laughter. "Inside me, I need you inside me!"

I pull back into a sitting position, taking my hands off her. I don't want to fuck her. I don't want to use that part of me, I'll feel like a man. Realization appears on her face and she sits up. "I'm sorry. I didn't think... Can you?"

"I doesn't get as hard as a man, but I can. I just...don't really like to."

She puts her hand over mine, stopping me from picking at my cuticle. "We don't have to...but I think we can do it in a way you'll like. Can we try? Can you trust me?"

It's what she wants. "Sure."

"Lay back, I'm going to fuck you."

She pulls my shorts down, straddles me and takes me into her wet opening, grinding her hips into mine. It's so warm, it feels so good, it's been so long. I grasp the sheets of the bed and arc my back with the building pleasure. The curve of my back inspires her, and she withdraws to grab my ankles and push my legs backward until they're locked behind my head. I gasp with the delight of being controlled. She takes me into her again, slamming her pelvis up and down, causing my bruises to cry out with the impact. But I love it. She's so aggressive, and in this position, it feels like I'm being fucked, entered, opened, taken to the brink of being torn apart.

My entire body gets warmer and warmer as the ecstasy of being ravaged builds. I throw my head back and close my eyes. She's grinding faster, I'm getting close to cumming, and I feel as if my body is covered in openings for her. A wetness increases between us. Wait.

I open my eyes, the pores all over my skin have grown and are dilating and quivering with the waves of pleasure, seeping out a clear, iridescent liquid. I open my mouth to scream, but she shoves her palm over my face and brings herself closer. Her naked body slides over mine, our curves slipping up and over each other with the lubrication of the slick, rainbow liquid. I close my eyes again and focus on our bodies gliding together, the wetness between us growing with my building orgasm.

She pants deeply and rhythmically, each breath growing louder until she screams. I can't tell if it sounds like she's reveling in a revenge murder—or she's the victim of a murder herself. It's so loud—it must be waking up neighbors, and I hear dogs bark in the distance. Her screams turn into unhinged laughter, and just before the building of my pleasure wanes from shock, she takes my face in a vise grip and presses her lips to mine, panting as our tongues dance. She presses her body against me as if she's trying to subsume my essence, like we're having humanity's final fuck, and it takes me over the edge.

And I cum, riding wave after wave of orgasm, as the iridescence pours out of my body from every pore, soaking us, making us glistening human soap bubbles— oil slicks. The climax is endless.

—

I lay back in bed, small waves of ecstasy still rippling through my totally relaxed body. This moment is perfect. Nothing exists but this feeling. I close my eyes and sink into it. She gets out of bed to get a towel, and I continue to lay here, trying to hold on to this moment.

Are we going to be together now? I hope she wants a relationship, but I'm not sure if she's the committed type. I imagine us laughing over breakfast at a cute cafe. She pops in and throws me a towel. "I'll be right back."

I hug the towel and stare at the ceiling, remembering the events of the past month and what I've become. My eyes drift to the easy chair with the sketchbook on top of it. What does she see when she looks at me? I wipe the iridescent fluid off me, as much as I can. It comes away easy enough with my lack of body hair.

I put my clothes back on and sit down, turning over her sketchbook to see the drawing of me. It's disturbing—not because it looks like my freakish self, but because I've seen it before. I flip through the older pages of the sketchbook...it's filled with drawings of me. No, they aren't me. How could I have not seen this before? These are almost the same as the drawings she displayed at the gallery. I'm lightheaded and my ears are ringing. How is this possible? What's happening?

I hear talking in the next room. There's someone else here! I open the door and Rayna is standing next to Dr. Skurm, still shimmering from our sex and covered only by a towel. She sighs and looks down as Skurm takes out his syringe of bright green liquid and walks toward me. I can't believe she did this, I trusted her. Look at me, Rayna. Please, look at me.

As if she can read my mind, she looks up as Dr. Skurm takes my arm and injects me with the fluorescent solution. What's the point of struggling? He's won.

"This will put you to sleep so I can examine you before I administer the final treatment," he says with the tone of a routine doctor's visit.

I just want Rayna to explain, I want to understand, and I plead to her with my eyes. She sighs again. "I'm sorry, Isa. I like you, I really do. The wheels were already in motion, and I had to see how you'd turn out. And you turned out perfect. You're just how I imagined."

I'm dizzy and the room is spinning, blackness clouds my vision from all sides. I'm sinking into the void and losing my footing. I fall to my knees and Dr. Skurm stares down at me with perfect powder-white skin and a calculating gaze. As my vision blinks away, I hear Rayna say, "Treat her okay until the ceremony, won't you Dad?"

CHAPTER FOURTEEN

I wake up in a chair with my feet tied and my hands cuffed behind me. Whatever he injected me with must have knocked me out, and I'm in his basement or something. The room is dark and drab, concrete floors with grey metal walls, a single bulb hanging from a cord, a heavy door that's surely locked, some sort of work bench—big enough for a human body—and a cabinet that's definitely filled with some creepy surgical implements.

I need to get out of here. No time for confusion, no time for self pity, no time for exhaustion, I absolutely can not find out what Skurm has planned for me. The cuffs are tight around my wrists, but after relaxing I'm able to slip my hands out and untie my feet—it's not just that I'm double, triple, quadruple, whatever-jointed, my bones seem to be flexible as well.

The door is locked, of course. Is there any other way out of here? The air vent? It's much too small for a person, but maybe it's just enough space for a freak like me. I guess it's time to find out what this body can do.

My newfound height makes reaching the grate and taking it off easy. But I shouldn't try escaping without a weapon. I open the cabinet and it's full of surgical implements like I predicted. One of them almost looks like a meat cleaver with a saw-toothed edge. Maybe it's a bone saw? There's nowhere to store it on my body in these PJs, but I take it anyway.

I place the chair under the air vent and crawl in, holding the weapon as I lift myself up. I'm mashed and squished, like a caved in camping tent with tangled and flexed poles, but I fit. And I can wriggle my way forward, keeping the blade ahead of me. I just hope the next room isn't too far.

My bones ache from the strain of their flexibility being tested as I inch forward, trying not to puncture or squeeze any of my organs that are vulnerable without a regular skeletal structure. An amber light appears and grows brighter. Thank god—I've made it to the grate in the next room.

I shove open the grate and it pops off and clatters to the floor as I spill out of the vent into a heap, dropping the blade. Fuck, that was loud, I hope Skurm or his minions didn't hear that. Minions. Does he have minions? Other than his fucking daughter, who betrayed me?

I've landed on an opulent, red, Persian rug. The room is filled with antiques and lit with what looks like gas lamps. There's another person in here—no, it's my reflection in a mirror with an ornate frame. I shudder and recoil. On the wall to my left is a door that might be my way out of this mess. To my right is an old wooden desk with stacks of books and papers covered in scribbles. I try the door, it's locked. It has one of those old keyholes you can use to spy on people and lock from either side. Only darkness is visible through it, but maybe there's a key in the desk.

The contents of a tipped over bottle of red ink cover some of the notes and a white feather quill. It's still wet. I thumb through the scribbled notes, and I can't make sense of any of it, until I discover my name and Instagram handle written out and circled. They targeted me. There's no key or anything I could use to pick the lock on the desk or in the drawers.

Drawings, color photocopies of pages from occult books, old black and white photographs, and other memorabilia are pinned to the wall. One photograph is of two men in front of a ship of some sort; it's dated

1917. The man on the right, I swear that's Dr. Skurm. The same facial features, but in this he actually looks like a human being. How old is he? If this is him, he'd have to be at least a hundred and twenty years old. It can't be him, it must be one of his relatives or something. Some drawings are Rayna's and others look like her research material. I don't understand them, but they're full of symbolism: a man with a sun-head opposing a woman with a moon-head, swirling black clouds surrounding broken pieces of planets, dragons eating their own tails, peacocks and other birds, and elements I can't identify. I guess her father shares Rayna's passion for alchemy, but he actually believes in this stuff. And the ceremonial black robe hanging to the right of the desk confirms it: Skurm is some sort of occultist.

I remember Rayna said something about a ceremony. What was she talking about? Some sort of weird wedding or religious rite?

There's a large bookcase next to the mirror, maybe the key is on a shelf or hidden in a book. And even if the books aren't hiding a key, maybe they'll have some answers. They're antique, hardbound with fabric covers and embossed with their titles. Most of the spines are dusty, but one of them, *Alchemy, Ancient and Modern*, looks like it's taken out and read often. I pull on the spine, but the book stops halfway out, and I hear a metal clicking sound. The shelf rotates to reveal the green glow of the hidden room behind it. A secret passageway. You've got to be shitting me.

I pick up my weapon from the rug and go to investigate. The room is dark except for an emerald glow emanating from three different tanks. Floating in each one is a something that used to be a someone. One looks like a half-empty trash bag made of flesh with un-closing, bulging eyes. It's floating in the green fluid like a jelly fish at an aquarium. God, it's a complete mess. Is this where I'm going to end up in if I can't escape?

The tanks softly buzz.

The next looks like a humanoid reptile, a scaly man with a lizard's head. But he's not anatomically correct—smooth like a Ken doll. It's uninspired, but if a picture of it made it to the internet, the reptilian conspiracy theorists would have a field day.

The last one looks like a spider formed of human parts. Six human legs on a bulbous torso and two arms sandwiching a row of four breasts. The spider woman's head is down, her short black hair obscuring her face. I get closer to the glass. What did he do to her face? My breath makes fog on the window. The hum of the tank grows in my ears until...

Silence.

Her head snaps up and her six human eyes dart in all directions as bubbles flow out of her caved in mouth. She's still alive! I jump back, almost dropping my weapon. She's thrashing and banging against the tank, alternating between trying to force her way through the glass to give me a creepy death hug, and bashing the sides to escape and skitter off. She's making too much noise—she's going to give me away. Her efforts at smashing the tank fail, so she lets out a high-pitched scream. It's muffled by the fluid and glass, but it's still deafening. She's definitely going to give me away!

I press any button I can find on the nearby control panel, hoping one of them will shut her up. Black liquid oozes into the tank and descends on her. She turns her focus toward the blob lowering over her and her scream becomes jittered and panicked. The goo coats her body, restricting her thrashing, and weighing her down to the bottom of the tank. The smell of burning hair fills the air. The green liquid drains out, until a twitching mass of tar is left behind, choking and gasping for air. Dear god, what did I do? Did I just kill her? It's for the best. I can't imagine wanting to live like that, I did her a favor. Jesus Christ, I hope I did her a favor.

"What have you done?" Dr. Skurm says from the secret passageway. I was so entranced by the spider lady dying that I hadn't noticed him come in.

"I...I didn't mean to, I was just trying to..."

"You killed her. You're a murderer."

"No, it was an accident! It was just—wait. You're the one who made her a freaky spider, not me! This is on you. Look what you did to these people! Look what you did to me."

Skurm smiles, the green glow reflecting off his porcelain powdered skin. "You're my greatest work, Isa. My magnum Opus."

"Well your work fucking sucks!"

I scream in rage and leap on to him like a

grasshopper, propelled by my elastic bones. He's caught off guard, so I'm able to knock him over and put the blade to the wrist of his scalpel hand, while pinning him to the floor with my knees. I saw into his wrist. Turns out this is a bone saw, after all.

Skurm screams and writhes and tries to pull me off him, but I keep sawing. He'll never touch another woman again. I've sawed through his lab coat and into his skin, and blood is gushing out. I'm hitting muscle! Almost to the bone. Keep screaming Skurm, you sick fuck, I can barely feel you punching my back. I feel the blade hit bone and it's like a drug, this is...this is incredible! Faster, harder, up and down and up and down, tear the flesh, the wet ripping sound, the soft crunching, it's exquisite. And then the saw gives; I've sawed through the bone and the resistance is gone, making way for a smooth finish, like hitting a freshly paved road after driving on the shit streets of LA.

He's not screaming anymore, and his hand drops to the floor with a satisfying plop, its fingers shaking and twitching. Blood spills out of it, but it's not human blood. It's blue and sticky. The fingers of the hand claw at the ground and it inches itself away from me, like a semi-crushed spider trying to escape. The muscle tissue coming out of Skurm's stump is white and bulbous and pulsating like a grub. I look up at him and he smiles at me. He raises a syringe gun with a loaded vial of red liquid. He sticks me in the arm with the pinky-sized needle, emptying the solution into me, as he digs it deeper and whispers in my ear. "Rubedo."

Every blood vessel in my body bursts at once, and their contents seep through my skin, staining it crimson.

CHAPTER FIFTEEN

I guess he figured out that shackles don't work on me because he's got me in a cage. It doesn't have metal bars, it's more of tall a plexiglass display case. The room is dark, only partially lit by a small lamp on a nearby table. I'm naked except for a tight black bikini that digs into my flesh. I have no idea where I am, and I'm still groggy from whatever was in that syringe gun—the final treatment. I thought all of my blood vessels burst, but I'm still alive so that couldn't have happened. My skin is definitely a ruby color now, even in this low light I can see that. I wonder if I'm like a sponge, and if I press my arm, blood will seep out of my skin. Maybe all my blood vessels really did burst, and I've become a human tampon. Oh, the irony.

I press my finger into my arm, it's rubbery, not spongy—and no blood. Well, that's good news. Wait. Where's my dick? There's no lump in my bikini bottom. I pull the elastic band away from my stomach and awkwardly position my body so that the light from the lamp shines down my pants. No dick. No Balls. I stick my hand down there—it's just smooth like a doll, but with a small divot that must be where I'd pee from. After all that I've been through, I can't even begin to process how to feel about this development in my genital situation.

A man walks in through a door, light spills out of a hallway and shadows him. I can't see his face, but he's wearing a T-shirt and jeans. I'm able to stand—I've grown even taller, I'm towering over this guy. What am I, 7 feet now? And it's like this cage was custom built to encase my freakish height. I bang on the thick plexiglass with my palms. "Let me out of here!"

I can't tell if he can hear me. Is this thing sound proofed? The walls are super thick, they didn't even budge when I hit them. He pulls the cage forward—it's on wheels—and pushes me into the hall. I can't hear the wheels against the floor. I bang on the glass again. "Where are you taking me? Where am I?"

It's no use. He wheels me through the dingy off-yellow hallway and takes me through a door into another dim area. It's a stage behind a red curtain. There's a line of three plexiglass cages like mine before me, each with strange figures inside. As I'm wheeled by, I'm able to catch a glimpse of the other poor transformed souls.

The first is some sort of man-raven hybrid. Black feathers sprout out of the humanoid body, and the arms are wings. I can't tell if it still has its human hands, but as I roll by, it turns toward me and I can see its face—human but with a dark gray beak and beady black eyes. The next is a woman sitting crossed legged, her skin is smooth like glass and she's luminescent, giving off a soft white glow like a dim lamp. Her figure is like one of those plastic anime figurines, formed to be inhumanly over-sexualized with exaggerated curves. The third is wearing some sort of peach-colored cloak—no. Its skin drapes like a cloak, I can see the hair growing from it. Is that a large flap of skin, or the surface of its body? Its head is even more disturbing. It's the size and shape of a basketball, and it's covered in eyes with a small patch of brown hair on top. Are the eyes looking at me? Are they functional? They're blinking. And the last is me. I'm wheeled into position next to eyeball skin cloak. What an unnerving neighbor. But he was human once too, like me. He's still human, I'm still human. Aren't we?

The red curtain slides open and we're hit with blinding stage lights. There's clapping, muffled and barely audible from inside my cage. The seating area of the theater isn't large—it could fit maybe fifty people, and it's only about half full. Straight ahead in the middle of the audience is a sort of long desk lit by a spotlight. A woman and two men sit behind it, and each has a screen facing us, attached to the side of the desk and lined up with their seat. They're dressed in fancy clothes and have large colorful buttons in front of them. What is this? Are they judges? Is this some sort of twisted version of American Idol?

Wait...they look familiar. The woman is pale and blonde and wearing an off-the-shoulder white dress with bright red lipstick and the longest fake-eyelashes I've ever seen. Holy shit, that's Kimmi! What is she doing here? The fit guy next to her—is he a celebrity too? He has a shaved head and wears a navy suit with no tie. I swear I've seen those thick, white-rimmed circular glasses before. Isn't he a famous director? Danny Laker—that's his name. The massive white guy on the other side of her, he's famous too. He's that body builder who started Improved U. They make the supplements that my dad tried to sell me, and the classes and juice fasts and coffee alternatives that influencers are always plugging on social media.

It's hard to see who else is in the audience, except in the front row where I see Dr. Skurm's gleaming face. He's wearing what looks like a fancy suit—black, but no tie. He still has his right hand, like nothing happened, and rolls the fingers as if he knows I'm looking at it. And next to him is Rayna. What the hell is she wearing? Is that a ball gown? Gold sequins and spaghetti straps, low cut and long—it looks designer. Why are they dressed like they're at some sort of award show? She smiles and gives a slight wave. I scream and bang on the wall with my fists. "You fucking bitch! How could you do this to me!"

Why waste my energy? I don't think they can even hear me. I plop down and cover my face with my long fingers. Tears stream down my cheeks, and I can sense that stupid basketball head's eyes on me. What the fuck is happening? None of this makes any sense.

A man in a white suit holding a microphone steps into view from the edge of the stage and addresses the audience. He looks Greek or Italian or something and has a waxed black mustache that's curled at the ends. I can't make out what he's saying, but he's working the crowd and gesturing to us. The audience claps.

After a short speech, he walks in front of the bird guy and dramatically gestures to him. More clapping, but not as loud. The judges talk and the audience turns to them. The Improved U guy says something with a shit-eating grin and the audience bursts into laughter. He slams on a button and the screen lights up with an I. Kimmi returns his grin and slams a button. Her screen lights up with the Roman numeral for two. Danny Laker has his arms crossed. He puts his hand up to his chin and strokes it and speaks before pressing the button with one finger. His screen lights up with a II.

The crowd claps and the man in the white suit walks to the bioluminescent, anime statue girl. He introduces her and knocks on her glass, gesturing for her to stand up. She stands and seems to glow brighter. He makes a spinning motion with his finger. She obliges and turns in a circle to show her entire body, making eye contact with me on her way around, with no expression. She faces forward again, and the lights turn off to better show her glow. For a moment, she and I are the only ones in the room, like I'm gazing at a single sad star in the middle of a moonless sky. The lights turn on, the judges are discussing. In succession they press their buttons: the fitness guy gives a V, Kimmi gives a III, and movie director gives a IV. The audience claps.

The man in the white suit steps toward my neighbor, beach ball head. Before he can even give his introductory gesture, all the judges slam their buttons, giving him a I. Harsh. A man in the audience storms out of the theater as the judges and audience laugh.

The white suit guy comes up to my cage, looking at me with a stretched smirk. Dr. Skurm and Rayna are leaning forward, and Rayna's fingers interlace. I guess this is their big fucking moment.

The man knocks on the glass and gestures for me to stand. I cover my head in my hands and make my body as small as possible. Maybe they'll disappear, maybe I'll turn invisible. Through my fingers, I see Skurm and Rayna shift in their seats and glance at each other. The man gestures again, but I'm staying seated. I'm not here. This isn't happening. He takes out a small remote and presses a button, electrifying the floor and sending a shooting pain into my ass and legs. My body stands up before I can stop it with my stubbornness. The crowd claps.

He motions for me to spin around, so I do. Pathetic. The crowd is still clapping, Skurm and Rayna grin and turn to the audience and judges. The judges beam and nod at each other. They press their buttons, V, V, V. They clap and the two men stand up, others in the audience stand as well, their cheers are audible but muffled. Skurm and Rayna are hugging. She looks so happy. The whole audience is on their feet, even Kimmi, giving me a standing ovation. A perfect score for being the perfect freak.

Skurm and Rayna turn toward me, yelling something I can't make out and waving their arms like they're congratulating or thanking me. Rayna blows me a kiss, she has tears in her eyes. The red curtain closes.

It's dark except for the glow of freak #2, and in her light, I see a stagehand walk toward me. He takes control of the cage and wheels me out of the room, leaving the rest of them behind. We roll down the hall until he takes me into an elevator with B2 over the door. He presses the button to go to B5. We're underground, and now we're going deeper.

I doubt I'm going to some sort of after-party in my honor, at least not one I'd like to attend. I stare at the man with my palms to the glass, hoping he'll look up at me and realize I'm a human being, but he just looks at the closed elevator door. This is ride is taking forever, it's only supposed to be three floors down.

The elevator comes to a halt and the doors open to reveal a cavern-like tunnel, lit with a line of oil lamps mounted on its off-white and light-brown stony walls. Are we really in a cave? Or is this a set?

I'm wheeled down the tunnel into a massive opening. Hundreds of delicate stalactites hang from the ceiling and large stalagmites rise from the ground, flanking the path. I'm wheeled toward a small amphitheater carved out of the stone and lit by standing lamps. It faces an area to my right that's shrouded in darkness. This is definitely a real cave. How deep are we?

Twenty or so figures in black cloaks sit on the stone benches. I can see their suits and dresses underneath some of them—these are the same people from the twisted beauty pageant. What is this? Some sort of alchemy cult? They see me and stand up again, giving me a second standing ovation. I feel a tinge of pride. For what? I don't know, maybe it's just reflexive.

I'm rolled past them into the dark corner of the cave. There's the muted sound of a large metal latch, and the soft creaking of a hinge. I'm pushed over a threshold on to unpaved ground. The sound of a metal door slamming rings out behind me. The door must be heavy if I can hear it through the plexiglass.

All I can see are the cloaked figures sitting in the amphitheater behind a series of massive, spread-out bars that reach the ceiling, and there's a mesh cage over it, sealing the gaps that I could walk through. Great, another cage.

A mechanism releases, and the walls of my plexiglass case fall open. I'm grateful to be out, but my gut tells me my situation hasn't improved. Stumbling across the straw floor, I reach the bars covered by a mesh cage wall and bang my palms on it. "Let me out, you psychos! I participated in your twisted beauty pageant, now let me out! I'm a fucking human being!"

They ignore me and light candles, each one holding their own, and murmur a chant. I can make out some of their faces in the candlelight. Skurm is in the front row again with Rayna. They're wearing red cloaks instead of black, I guess that's the gold star they get for changing me into a prize-winning freak.

Their chanting grows louder, it's in a language I don't understand—maybe Latin. They raise their candles above their heads with thunderous voices that echo off the walls of the cavern, then fall silent in perfect unison. The cultists blow out their candles. The click of a large switch echoes in the cave. A man in overalls activated it, and it belongs to a control panel built into the cave wall next to the audience. Floodlights in the cage turn on, illuminating the space.

Opposite the cage wall is a large opening. It's unlit and I can't see inside. Strewn about are human bones and skulls, the one at my feet is distorted, lengthened with an enormous jaw. Some skulls and skeleton pieces are just as transformed, and others appear normal. This is bad.

Heavy breathing comes from the darkened opening. It's a beast for sure, but it's so loud—too loud for it to be the size of a normal animal like a lion. Footsteps accompany the breathing, sounding like a car being dropped, shaking the ground more and more as whatever-it-is gets closer. I run to the cage wall. The audience has their hoods off and I can see their faces. They're so excited, like they're watching the season finale of their favorite show. I'm surprised no one's selling popcorn or hotdogs. Skurm looks more self satisfied than anything, and Rayna—is she crying? If she regrets betraying me, maybe she can help. I grab the mesh of the cage as the booming footsteps get closer. "Rayna, help! Save me, please! I don't want to die! I don't want to die!"

A hot gust of wind hits my back, followed by a horrible, deafening sound, like the death rattle of a hundred elephants. I turn around and at the tunnel entrance is a 50 foot...thing. It's taller than my three-story apartment building! I can't believe what I'm seeing. Its torso is the shape of a giant chicken, but it's covered in scales, and the wings are webbed and reptilian. It has a tail four times the length of its body that looks like a snake. Sprouting from its torso are three long goose-like necks, each topped with a different bird's head—one black like a crow, one white like a swan, and one red.

What's in the middle of the beast's chest is registering with me, and I blink my eyes and shake my head to make sure I'm seeing what I think I'm seeing. Most of the beast's front side is covered by the massive scowling face of an old man with a pointy nose and chin, and a long beard that almost reaches the ground. And if that wasn't absurd enough, its human-like legs are half-red and don't have toes—they look like little red boots and have wings sprouting from the ankles. I'm dreaming, I must be dreaming, this can't be real, it's too insane.

The monster's old man face flares its nostrils and sniffs at me, as the three bird heads weave and bob through the air on their long necks, scoping out the area. The thing roars from the face, and that Godzilla-with-strep-throat sound bursts out from its toothless mouth and hits me with a wave of hot breath and spit. My head swims from the foul smell of decay. This is no dream. This is some ancient THING that those maniacs out there summoned, and I'm the sacrifice. Or they just get their kicks watching a freak in a bikini get eaten alive by some fantasy monster. Either way, I'm fucked.

Its snake-tail whips and strikes me in the side. The force sends me flying to the corner, and I land on a pile of bones and skulls. A crusty broken rib in the pile pierces my side, but the wound is only superficial. The beast is stomping toward me, its bird heads now as focused on me as its old man face.

I'm not fucked. This is a final boss, and every final boss can be defeated. I just have to figure out its patterns and find its weakness. I pick up a bone from the pile and hurl it at the monster. It rotates through the air and bounces off the massive brow—so close to the eye. The face twists into an annoyed expression, but the beast doesn't stop stepping toward me.

I pick up a skull, it looks human but with sabretooth fangs. I stand and wind back my throwing arm, but the middle bird head, the one with red feathers, winds back too. It looks like it's going to scream or strike or—the beast's body tips down and the red bird head charges toward me, straightening its serpentine neck taught. I spring up and roll away with the skull just before the beak slams into the corner of the wall where I stood. I run behind the creature, trying to stay away from the lashing tail. The red bird head chews on the pile of straw and bones, and the pieces fall out on to the floor as it turns toward me. The old man face looks super pissed, and it lets out monstrous grunts.

I can do this. Focus. I throw the skull into the eye of its human face, and the sabre teeth burrow deep into the bulging eyeball. Yes! The beast sways from side to side while it groans and blinks, trying to dislodge the skull from its eye. The bird heads crane down, assessing if they can safely pull the skull out with their beaks. That middle one with the red feathers seems like it's in charge, maybe if I kill it, I can survive this.

I pick up an oversized rib from the ground and slip it behind my back under the elastic band of the bikini. Running toward the beast, I jump on to the beard, gripping it with my hands and putting one hand over another to climb up to its chin. The creature shakes its body from side to side, wagging the beard and swinging me like someone trying to get a bug off their sleeve. And like a bug, I hold on tight and climb up every moment that the beard is stable enough. The pointy end of the rib jabs into my back with the movement. Cheers and boos ring out from the audience.

The beast is still. I dig my nails into the flesh of its chin and pull myself up until I'm crouching on top of it. These new joints are finally making sense. I can do this. I grasp the massive bottom lip, squeezing lumps of its blueish flesh. The white bird head is trying to pick the skull out of its human eye, the red bird has its sights on me and looks pissed, and the black bird...is coming right at me!

I scramble up the lip and into the foul, toothless mouth. At least I hope its toothless. The gums of the creature clamp down, and the wet flaps engulf my body. I squirm and scramble to grab its pulsating tongue as it grinds me between its gums, clamping down harder and harder. If my bones weren't flexible, they'd have broken from the force. It's swallowing and the suction is pulling me deeper into the mouth. I grasp for something, anything to hold on to so I'm not eaten alive. The beast has a tooth after all—it's the size of a large suitcase, and I wrap my arms around it, finding handholds in two cavities. The monster draws my body back and lashes at me with its tongue as I hold on tight. I let myself go limp while keeping my grip on the tooth, and my body flails with the motion of the tongue without resistance.

I wonder what would happen if I just let go? Would it hurt? Would it hurt to slip into the mouth of a monster and disappear forever? If I never want to be seen again anyway, why fight it?

The tongue stops and the old man face of the monster screams in frustration. I force myself out of its mouth, back on to its chin and jump with my hands up toward the nose, catching a long nose hair and the edge of a nostril. The crowd gasps. I lift myself to the top of the nose and straddle it before the creature shakes its body again. But I hold tight... It's just like a bull machine at a bar. I can do this.

The beast is still for a moment, making a sound like it's trying to clear its old man throat. Scrambling to my feet, I run up the slope of the nose and lunge off the brow, landing on the base of the neck of the red bird head. The feathers make it easy to climb, and I'm fast enough to dodge a strike from the beak of the black bird. I'm at the base of the head. I steady myself as I feel for the weapon on my back. Shit. It's gone. It fell out when I was in the mouth!

I'll have to use my long, freaky arms and fingers. I

pull myself up on to the beak and plunge my arms into its eye socket, grasping the sides of its beach ball sized, black eyeball in my hands. The eye detaches as I pull at it with all my strength. The bird head screeches and tips back and I tumble off hugging the massive eyeball. I drop it and pull at feathers to slow my descent before I land, bouncing off the squishy bird eye on the ground below me. It cushions my fall, but the impact still rattles my body with pain.

The beast is freaking out, spasming and shaking. It regains composure and spins, charging toward me, and the red bird head strikes with its beak. I turn and it barely misses me. It plummets into the cavern wall, causing it to cave-in and shards of stone to fly out. Holy shit, this thing is pissed. It's blinded by rage—and maybe I can use this to my advantage.

I run around the beast to the giant bars and mesh wall of the cage, and turn to face it, positioning my body in the center of two of the massive bars. I give my best crow imitation. "Caw! Caw!"

It works. The sharp beak flies toward me, and at the last second, I collapse to the floor. It hits the mesh metal wall above me and tears a hole through it. A woman screams. The monster wriggles somewhat, its beak and head stuck in the hole it created. It yanks its head out, and I stand and dive through the opening, out of the cage. I'm free!

And I'd be celebrating if there wasn't a crowd of cultists staring at me in shock, regaining their composure at any moment. The massive sound of rattling cage bars and the monstrous body thumping against them snaps the cultists out of their confusion. The front row rushes forward with their arms out to restrain me—except Skurm and Rayna, who're still dumbfounded. Others jump over stone seats to join the party. They're grabbing, grappling, grasping at me, but they can't get a hold of me. My body is too slick from the monster's saliva, and I can bend and flex away with ease. I swim amid the mass of arms and legs and torsos and make my way through. A hand squeezes the back of my neck and pulls me around. It's that Improved U guy, and the grip of his huge hand is so strong—I can't get out of it. He knows he has me and gives me a nasty grin. I make eye contact with the monster and squeeze out another crow call. "Caw caw!"

The monster tips down and forces its red bird head through the hole in the bars. The beak plummets through the cultists toward me, knocking them to the ground and into the air. I fall on to my back and push up the Improved U guy with my feet. He's scooped up into the beak, and it releases his grip by severing his arm as it engulfs his body. He's crushed into a bloody pulp, and the sound of his breaking bones escapes the bird's mouth.

I scramble to my feet and bolt up the side of the amphitheater toward the control panel, grabbing a standing lamp, smashing its glass globe to make a staff with an end of sharp glass. I'm so much faster with these long, springy limbs. Cultists from the second row charge toward me, led by Danny Laker, and I plunge my weapon into his chest at the same time the creature slams into the cage wall. He falls back, knocking the rest over in a domino effect. Another is rushing me from above, I turn my body and swing the lamp, hitting him in the head with the metal base. The next one I stab in the face. I'm reach the control panel. The workman yells at me from across the cave. "No! Don't touch that!"

I flip every switch I see and then smash it with the lamp. The sound of the massive latch of the cage door unlocking reverberates, followed by the horrified gasps of the cultists. Three cultists jump on top of me, but I squirm free from the dog pile to see the monster bursting out of the gate. The huge cage door swings open and slams into at least half of the cultists sending them flying like bowling pins. Skurm and Rayna escape the path of the cage, but the monster is heading right for them as the bird heads snatch up cultists, crushing them in their beaks and feeding their mashed up bodies to the old man face, who slurps down the remains into his toothless mouth with delight.

The black bird head scoops up Skurm in its beak as the red one goes for Rayna. She's fast enough to get away, but Skurm isn't as lucky, the beast bites down on his body and shakes its head, sending the top half of the doctor flying to the floor. He lands with a thunk and yellow and white guts spill out in a rush of blue fluid, and dangle from the bottom of his severed torso. Rayna turns toward him and screams. He lifts his head, a massive crack is across his face. The fracture branches at his forehead, and a shard of the surface falls off, leaving a hole with only blackness behind it. He crawls to her, clawing at the cave floor, and reaches his hand out.

Someone is at my right shoulder. I whip back my arm with my pivoting joint and hit something with a crack. It's Kimmi, and she's holding her bloody nose. I push her to the ground. "I looked up to you! I danced to your music and dreamed about buying your clothes!"

Her eyes are wide in terror, she's stuttering. I turn back to the monster. "Caw! Caw!"

I bolt for the tunnel that leads to the elevator as the creature charges forward, its old man face twisted in rage. The surviving cultists follow, at this point they probably aren't as interested in catching me as much as they want to escape. But I'm a good 15 feet ahead of them. The beast is behind us and gaining fast, I hear the screams of the people crushed under the ridiculous red boot-like feet of the monster and torn apart by its beaks.

The cave ceiling tapers down toward the tunnel and the monster bashes into the lower hanging stalactites. Rocks crash to the ground in a hail of stone behind me as I jump into the tunnel. I'm in, I did it. I turn as I run and stop when I see the opening—it's covered in large stone debris. And there's...silence. I'm panting, trying to catch my breath. I think I did it.

Rocks fly toward me, propelled by the massive red bird head jamming its way into the tunnel, and a rock the size of a toaster strikes me in the shoulder, knocking me down. The open, sharp beak of the red bird's head rushes toward me. I scream and cover my face. This is it.

But it stops short. Its neck isn't long enough to

reach me. I run to the elevator and jam the up button. The door opens and I rush in, smashing the B2 button. The door closes as the red bird head thrashes and screeches, banging itself on the walls of the tunnel, smashing the gas lamps on the wall, letting out splatters of fire.

I made it. I'm getting out of here. But not before I find the others.

CHAPTER SIXTEEN

Droplets of rain patter against my black umbrella. Kind of cliche for it to rain at my dad's funeral, but I guess life is cliche sometimes. People in LA always say 'We need the rain' even if they don't like it, because it's so rare. I walk across the squishy grass toward the small group of people surrounding his open grave at the back of the cemetery grounds. I must look like a grim reaper, towering in my long black dress that covers all my skin, and the hood with a veil covering my freakish face. This umbrella, my scythe.

I almost didn't come. Dealing with my new appearance and the trauma of escaping whatever the fuck Skurm and his creepy buddies had planned for me has been a full-time job. But I'd regret it if I didn't say goodbye. The dad I loved and understood left me a long time ago, but now I know he's never coming back.

I'm getting closer and can make out the attendees.

Almost everyone from my dad's side of the family is there, some of his friends, and some strangers. Among my family is cousin Rick, the dubious human known as Uncle Tommy, Aunt Cleo and her two little girls, the other aunts, and other family members whose names and relations I can't remember. And of course, my sister. My mom and her side of the family are absent, which is no surprise. The mourners turn toward me, like they can sense my presence. They're nervous, expectant. Except my sister, Sarah, she's almost smiling. Out of pity?

Do they all know? Do they know who I am and what's happened to me? They must. Everyone knows; everyone has heard the rumors of my monstrous form. What do they see when they think of me? And who will they see if they peer under this veil?

I can't control it. I can't control what they'll see and how they'll think about me. What's the point of hiding?

I stand next to Sarah in front of the grave, all their eyes are on me, even the priest at the front who I've never met. He's holding his book like he was ready to start before I arrived and made a scene. Drops fall into the open grave and land on the slick surface of my father's coffin. Why am I afraid to be seen by strangers who mean nothing to me? Why should I be scared for my family to find out what I look like? They already didn't accept me after I came out as trans.

The rain is turning to a drizzle, and the sun is coming out. I put down my umbrella and remove my veil and hood.

There's a collective gasp. The two little girls start

screaming and crying, trying to pull away from their mother, pleading her to let them run from the monster. The priest's eyes dart back to his Bible and he begins to mutter a prayer under his breath. The rest of the faces of the amorphous blob of my extended family twist and grimace in disgust, gagging and groaning like they ate a rotten pistachio. Uncle Tommy shakes his head at me, as if to say *how could you do this*.

My sister looks at me with her hands over her mouth. Like she's trying to smile in support while holding her vomit.

I laugh to myself, and lift my head to feel the sun on my face and the last few drops of rain.

CHAPTER SEVENTEEN

My needle vibrates into the virgin skin, depositing its red ink with a satisfying buzz. I'm entranced by its movement as I drag it across my customer's rib, tattooing the image of a melting clown face. Mitzy is going to freak when I tell her a fan is getting a tattoo of one of her paintings. I'm so proud of that bitch.

"Ow!" he says.

I swipe off the excess ink and resume tattooing. "Hold still. I warned you about getting your first on your ribs."

He groans. "I don't think I can take it anymore. I can't do this."

"You can do it, buddy. You've waited almost a year and dropped a couple grand to let me do this to you."

He groans in agony. "I can't, I can't. I'm tapping out."

I dig into his skin with just a teeny bit more pressure. He should have listened. "No refunds, you sure you want to be a quitter?"

"Can I please just take a break?"

I lift the tattoo gun from his skin. "Of course, get yourself some water and chill on the couch for a few minutes."

The kid wanders off, and I check my equipment and wipe my nose-hole with a tissue before swigging my water bottle. The bell attached to the front door of my shop jingles. A tall woman walks in holding a cylindrical briefcase, like a box for a top hat with a handle on it. Put my water down. "Sorry, we don't take walk-ins. You'll— holy shit. Rayna?"

Rayna looks me up and down, checking out my body mods: my gauged ears, my sub-dermal implants, the piercings all over my face and body, and of course my killer tattoos. Once my red skin faded to an Irish-colored blush, and I was able to gain back some weight, I had to put my mark on it. I covered my canvas with demons from every culture, and all the classic Hollywood monsters—like the Wolf Man, Dracula, Creature from the Black Lagoon, Frankenstein's Monster. Rayna smiles, revealing a missing tooth. "Hello, Isa."

"What're you doing here? It's been years, I figured you were dead."

She sits down in the tattoo chair across from me, putting the cylindrical case on her lap and folding her hands over it. "I kept seeing articles about you pop up online. When I saw you on the cover of Body Mod Magazine and heard about your new shop, I knew we had to reconnect. You aren't on social media, so I decided to come visit in person."

"I wish you hadn't."

She smiles, and I have to remind myself she's evil, because somehow her missing tooth makes her even more cute. "I wanted to congratulate you. This place is fantastic, and you've had so much success and recognition in such a short time."

"Yea, well thanks to you, I'm kind of hard to ignore." The nerve of her showing up here after she betrayed me, condemned to death-by-fantasy-monster.

She grins, the gap from her missing tooth peaks out and her deformed nose crinkles. My heart melts despite myself. Goddammit. Why is she still so hot? Why am I still so attracted to her? Rayna takes her hand off the top of the case and touches my leg. It's warm. She's not wearing her yellow contacts, and I gaze into her warm brown eyes. She squeezes my leg and returns her hand to the case when I flinch. "I've missed you."

"I can't say the same. But...before I kick you out of my shop, I have to know what that thing in the cave was."

She's thinking. "Well...the legend tells that The Beast was once human, like you. The great alchemists of antiquity held a contest to see who could transmute a human subject into the most fearsome monster. Adonis Mercurious, fabled to be a disciple of Hermes Trismegistus himself, showed unique dedication to the challenge. He locked himself in a cave with his equipment for forty days and forty nights, where he channeled powers and discovered formulas unmatched in their brilliance, even today. The result was The Beast, a superb celestial amalgamation of man, dragon, and fowl, representing every stage of the alchemical process. Mercurious' presented his creation at the contest, and it triumphed over the competition, but it cost him his life. He was devoured by his own creation soon after. The contest still continues to this day, as you've experienced. It's evolved with the times, but in honor of the first champion, Mercurious, the winning subject each year must face-off with his creation."

She sounds like Skurm, like she's retelling it from memory. Does she actually think that ridiculous story is true? I wonder how young she was when she first heard it. I lean back and cross my arms. "Sure. And does your little club still hold its annual contest?"

"Of course."

But it wasn't Rayna who said that. It came from her direction, but she didn't open her mouth. And it sounded garbled and artificial.

Rayna smirks at my confused expression and reaches to a latch on the side of the case, swinging open the front of it. Inside is a tank of green fluid with the cracked porcelain head of Skurm suspended in it. "Dad's missed you too, Isa."

Skurm's eyes arrest me with his gaze. A hideous smile grows on his face. Acrid green smoke pours out of vents from the bottom of the tank, and I cough as it invades my lungs. I'm getting lightheaded and this horrible sound like an ape drowning won't stop. He's laughing. He's laughing.

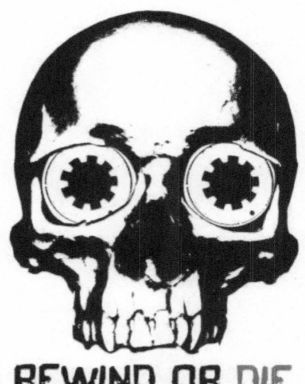

REWIND OR DIE

REWIND OR DIE

Made in the USA
Las Vegas, NV
06 December 2023